THE ADVENTURES
OF TOM SAWYER

BY

MARK TWAIN

SIMPLIFIED BY
W. J. HOGGETT, B.A.

LONGMAN

LONGMAN GROUP LIMITED
London

Associated companies, branches and representatives
throughout the world

© Longman Group Ltd 1949

First published in this series 1949
New impressions *1959; *1961; *1962 (twice);
*1963 (twice); *1964 (twice); *1965;
*1966 (twice); *1967; *1968; *1969 (thrice);
*1970; *1971 (twice); *1972;
*1973; *1974; *1975;
*1977

ISBN 0 582 52875 5

The Publishers are indebted to the Mark Twain Company,
New York, for permission to issue this simplified edition.

Printed in Great Britain by
Hazell Watson & Viney Ltd, Aylesbury

LONGMAN SIMPLIFIED ENGLISH

SERIES

This book has been specially prepared to make enjoyable reading for people to whom English is a second or a foreign language. An English writer never thinks of avoiding unusual words, so that the learner, trying to read the book in its original form, has to turn frequently to the dictionary and so loses much of the pleasure that the book ought to give.

This series is planned for such readers. There are very few words used which are outside the learner's vocabulary.[1] These few extra words are needed for the story and are explained when they first appear. Long sentences and difficult sentence patterns have been simplified. The resulting language is good and useful English, and the simplified book keeps much of the charm and flavour of the original.

At a rather more difficult level there is *The Bridge Series,* which helps the reader to cross the gap between the limited vocabulary and structures of the *Simplified English Series* and full English.

It is the aim of these two series to enable thousands of readers to enjoy without great difficulty some of the best books written in the English language, and in doing so, to equip themselves in the pleasantest possible way, to understand and appreciate any work written in English.

[1]The 2,000 root words of the *General Service List of English Words* of the *Interim Report on Vocabulary Seleetion.*

CONTENTS

CHAPTER 1

"FULL OF MISCHIEF"

"Tom!"

No answer.

"Tom!" cried Aunt Polly again.

No answer.

"I wonder where that boy's gone. Tom!"

The old lady pulled her spectacles down on her nose and looked over them about the room. Then she put them up and looked out under them. She seldom or never looked through them for so small a thing as a boy. She seemed puzzled for a moment and said:

"Well, if I catch you, I'll——"

She did not finish, for by this time she was bending down and pushing the sweeping-brush under the bed. She disturbed nothing but the cat. Then she went to the open door and looked out in the garden. Tom was not in sight.

"To-o-o-m!" she shouted.

There was a slight noise behind her, and she turned just in time to seize a small boy and prevent him from running away.

"What have you been doing in that cupboard?"

"Nothing."

"Nothing! Look at your hands, and look at your mouth. What *is* that stuff?"

"*I* don't know, aunt."

"Well, *I* know. It's jam.[1] I've told you forty times that if you touched that jam I'd skin you. Hand me that stick."

The blow was about to fall.

[1] Jam = fruit boiled with sugar.

"Hi! Look behind you, aunt!"

The old lady whirled round and snatched her skirts out of danger. The boy fled, and disappeared over the high fence of the garden. His aunt stood surprised for a moment, and then gave a gentle laugh.

"Hang the boy! Can't I ever learn anything? Hasn't he played that trick before? He's full of mischief, but he's my own dead sister's boy, poor thing, and I hate whipping[1] him. Every time I hit him my old heart almost breaks, and every time I forgive him my conscience blames me. He'll stay away from school this afternoon, and I'll be obliged to punish him by making him work to-morrow. It's cruel to make him work on a Saturday, when all the boys are having a holiday, but he hates work more than anything else, and I must do my duty towards the child, or I'll spoil his character."

Tom did stay away from school, and he had a very good time. He returned just in time to help Jim, the small servant boy, to saw and split the next day's firewood before supper. Tom's younger brother (or rather stepbrother), Sidney, had already finished his part of the work, for he was a quiet boy, and had no adventurous, troublesome ways.

While Tom was eating his supper and stealing sugar every time he had an opportunity, Aunt Polly was wondering whether Tom had disobeyed her and had been to the river. She had sewn up his shirt at the neck in order to prevent him from taking it off and swimming.

"Tom, it was quite warm in school, wasn't it? Didn't you want to go swimming?"

"No, auntie. Well, not much."

"Come here. Show me your collar."

Tom opened his coat. The neck-band of his shirt was securely sewn.

---

[1] A whip = a stick with a string on the end; to whip = to beat with a whip or a stick.

"Well, you may go out and play. I was sure that you had stayed away from school and been swimming."

"I thought you sewed his collar with white thread," said Sidney. "Now it's black."

"Why, I did sew it with white thread! Tom!"

But Tom did not wait for the rest. As he went out he said, "Sid, I'll give you a beating for that."

In a safe place Tom examined two needles which were stuck in his coat. One needle had white thread wound round it and the other had black.

"She wouldn't have noticed it, but for Sid. Hang it, sometimes she sews it with white and sometimes she sews it with black. I can't remember which she uses. I wish she'd stick to one colour. But I'll make Sid suffer for that."

Within two minutes he had forgotten all his troubles. A stranger was standing before him, a boy a little bigger than himself. A stranger of any age, male or female, was an object of curiosity in the poor little village of St. Petersburg. This boy was well dressed, too—well dressed on a week-day. Tom stared scornfully at the stranger's fine clothes, which seemed to make his own appear worn-out. Neither boy spoke. Finally, Tom said:

"I can beat you!"

"I'd like to see you try it."

"Well, I can do it."

"No you can't."

"Yes I can."

"No you can't"

"I can."

"You can't."

"Can."

"Can't."

An uncomfortable pause followed. Then Tom drew a line in the dust with his big toe, and said:

"You daren't step over that. If you do, I'll beat you till you can't stand up."

The new boy at once stepped over the line, and said:
"Now let me see you do it."

"You had better be careful."

"Well, you *said* you'd do it. Why don't you do it?"

"For two cents I *will* do it."

The new boy took two coins out of his pocket, and held them out scornfully.

Tom struck them to the ground.

In an instant both boys were rolling in the dirt, fighting like cats. For a few minutes they tore at each other's hair and clothes, hit and scratched each other's noses, and covered themselves with dirt and glory. At last through the dust of battle Tom appeared, sitting on the new boy and striking him with his fists.

"Say that you've had enough!" said Tom.

The boy only struggled to free himself.

"Say 'Enough!'"

The hitting went on.

Finally the stranger gasped "Enough!" Tom let him get up, and said, "Now that will teach you."

The new boy went off brushing the dust from his clothes, occasionally looking back and threatening what he would do to Tom the next time he met him. Tom replied with insults. As soon as Tom's back was turned the new boy snatched up a stone, threw it, and hit Tom between the shoulders. Then he ran like a deer. Tom chased the traitor home, and thus found out where he lived. He then held a position at the gate for some time, daring the enemy to come outside; but the enemy only made faces at him through the window, and refused. At last the enemy's mother appeared, and called Tom a vicious, impolite child, and ordered him to go away.

Tom got home late that night, and when his aunt saw the state of his clothes, she became more determined than ever to make him work hard during the holiday on Saturday.

CHAPTER 2

THE FENCE IS WHITEWASHED

SATURDAY morning had come and all the world was bright and fresh. There was a song in every heart, cheerfulness in every face, and a spring in every step.

Tom appeared on the pavement with a bucket of whitewash and a long-handled brush. He regarded the fence thoughtfully, and his heart was filled with despair. Thirty yards of fence nine feet high! It seemed to him that life was not worth living and that existence was only a burden. Sighing, he dipped his brush into the bucket and passed it along the topmost board; repeated the operation; did it again; compared the trifling whitewashed strip with the immensity of unwhitewashed fence, and sat down on a box discouraged.

Jim came dancing out at the gate with a bucket, singing. Before this, bringing water from the town pump had always been hateful work in Tom's opinion, but now it did not seem so. He remembered that there was company at the pump. Boys and girls were always there, waiting their turns, resting, exchanging playthings, quarrelling, fighting, and fooling about. He remembered that, although the pump was only a hundred and fifty yards away, Jim never got back with a bucket of water in less than an hour. Even then somebody generally had to go after him.

" I say, Jim," said Tom, " I'll fetch the water if you'll whitewash a bit."

Jim shook his head.

" I can't, Master Tom. The Mistress told me not to stay fooling about with anyone."

" Oh, never mind what she said, Jim. Give me the bucket. I won't be a minute. She won't know."

"Oh, I daren't, Master Tom. She would tear my head off. She would really."

"She never hurts anybody. She just gives them a little slap. And who cares about that? Jim, I'll give you a marble."[1]

Jim was only human. This temptation was too much for him. He put down the bucket and took the marble. In another minute he was flying down the street with the bucket. Tom was whitewashing energetically, and Aunt Polly was returning to the house with a slipper in her hand and a triumphant gleam in her eye.

But Tom's energy did not last. He began to think of the fun he had planned for this day. Soon, he thought, the free boys would come hurrying along on all sorts of delightful trips, and they would laugh at him for having to work. The very thought of it burnt him like fire. He got out and examined his worldly wealth. It consisted of bits of toys, marbles and rubbish, and was not enough to buy even half an hour of pure freedom.

At this dark and hopeless moment he had an idea—a glorious idea.

He took the brush and went calmly to work. Presently Ben Rogers, whose mockery he had been dreading most, came in sight. In his hand there was a fine apple. Tom went on whitewashing and paid no attention to him. Ben stared a moment, and then said:

"Hi! You're in trouble, aren't you!"

There was no answer. Tom regarded his last touch with the eye of an artist. Then he gave his brush another gentle sweep, and inspected the result as before. Ben came nearer. Tom's mouth watered for the apple, but he stuck to his work.

"Hello, Tom!" said Ben. "You have to work, eh?"

"Why, it's you, Ben! I didn't notice you."

"I say, I'm going swimming. Don't you wish you

---

[1] A marble=a small stone or glass ball played with by children.

could come? But of course you'd rather work, wouldn't you? Of course you would!"

Tom eyed the boy thoughtfully.

"What do you call work?"

"Why, isn't that work?"

Tom filled his brush with whitewash, and answered carelessly:

"Well, perhaps it is, and perhaps it isn't; but it suits Tom Sawyer."

"What! Do you mean to say that you like it?"

The brush continued to move.

"Like it? Well, I don't see why I shouldn't like it. A boy doesn't get a chance every day to whitewash a fence."

Ben had never thought of this before. He took a bite out of his apple. Tom swept his brush artistically to and fro. Then he stepped back to note the effect. He added a touch here and there, and criticized the effect again. Ben was watching every move, and getting more and more interested.

"I say, Tom, let me whitewash a bit," said Ben presently.

Tom considered, and was about to consent; but he changed his mind.

"No! No! You see, Aunt Polly's very particular about this fence. It's facing the street, you know. If it was the back fence I wouldn't mind, and she wouldn't. Yes, she's very particular about this fence. It must be done very carefully. I don't think there's one boy in a thousand, perhaps two thousand, who can do it in the way it has to be done."

"Is that so? How interesting! Let me just try, only just a little. I'd let you, if you were me, Tom."

"Ben, I'd like to, really; but Aunt Polly wouldn't like it. Jim wanted to do it, but she wouldn't let him. Sid wanted to do it, but she wouldn't let Sid. Now, don't you see that I'm responsible? If you started to whitewash this fence, and anything went wrong——"

"Oh, nonsense; I'll be very careful. Now let me try. I say, I'll give you my apple when I've nearly finished it."

"Well—no, Ben, I mustn't. I'm afraid——"

"I'll give you all of it."

Tom gave up the brush with unwillingness in his face but eagerness in his heart. While Ben worked and sweated in the sun, the retired artist sat on a barrel in the shade close by, ate his apple, and planned the downfall of more innocent victims. Boys arrived frequently. They came to mock, but remained to whitewash. By the time Ben was tired out, Tom had promised the next chance to Billy Fisher for a kite in good repair. When Billy retired, Johnny Miller bought his place for a dead rat and a string to swing it with. Thus the work went on, hour after hour.

By the middle of the afternoon, Tom was wealthy. He had, besides the things mentioned above, twelve marbles, a pair of spectacles without glasses, a piece of blue bottle-glass to look through, a key that would not unlock anything, a piece of chalk, a tin soldier, two tiny frogs, a little cat with only one eye, a brass door-handle, a dog-collar, the handle of a knife, and an old window-frame. He had had a nice, idle time and plenty of company, and the fence had three coats of whitewash on it. If he had not run short of whitewash, he would have stripped every boy in the village of his proudest possessions.

Tom said to himself that life was worth living after all. He had discovered, without knowing it, this great law of human action: in order to make a man or a boy desire a thing, it is only necessary to make the thing difficult to obtain.

CHAPTER 3

JOYS AND SORROWS

TOM stood before Aunt Polly. The soft summer air, the restful quiet, the scent of the flowers and the sleepy murmur of the bees had had their effect, and she was nodding in her armchair. Her spectacles were up on her grey head for safety. She thought that Tom had deserted long ago, and she wondered to see him place himself in her power again in this bold way.

"May I go out and play now, auntie?" he said.

"What, already? How much have you done?"

"It's all done, auntie."

"Tom, don't lie to me. I hate lies."

"I'm not lying, auntie. It *is* all done."

Aunt Polly could hardly believe this, and went out to see for herself. She would have been content to find a quarter of Tom's statement true. When she found the entire fence whitewashed, and not only whitewashed but carefully coated and recoated, she gasped with astonishment.

"Well, I never! I must say you *can* work when you try, Tom. But it's seldom that you do try. Well, run along and play."

She was so astonished at Tom's performance that she took him to the cupboard and picked out the finest apple for him.

He danced out into the garden and saw Sid. In a moment the air was full of lumps of earth. They flew round Sid's ears, and before Aunt Polly could come to the rescue six or seven had hit him and Tom was over the fence and gone. There was a gate, but generally he was too short of time to make use of it. He was satisfied, since he had punished Sid for calling attention to the black thread and getting him into trouble.

As he was passing the house where Jeff Thatcher lived, he saw a new girl in the garden. She was a lovely little blue-eyed angel with two long tails of yellow hair. At once a girl called Amy Lawrence vanished completely out of Tom's heart.

He worshipped this new angel till he saw that she had discovered him. Then he pretended that he did not know she was present, and began to act in all sorts of silly boyish ways in order to win her admiration. While he was in the midst of some dangerous tricks, he glanced[1] aside and saw that the little girl was going towards the house. Tom came up to the fence and leaned on it, hoping that she would wait a little longer. Tom sighed as she put her foot on the doorstep, but his face lit up at once, for she threw a rose over the fence just before she disappeared. The boy ran round, picked up his treasure, and buttoned it inside his coat next to his heart, or next to his stomach possibly, for he was not quite sure where the one began and the other ended.

All through supper he was so gay that his aunt wondered why. She scolded him for throwing lumps of earth at Sid, but he did not seem to mind in the least. He tried to steal sugar under his aunt's very nose, and got a tap on his fingers with a spoon.

"Aunt, you don't hit Sid when he takes sugar," he said.

"Well, Sid doesn't worry me as you do. You would be always stealing sugar if I didn't watch you."

Sid smiled in a self-satisfied way, and when the old lady went into the kitchen he reached for the sugar-basin. But his fingers slipped, and the basin dropped and broke. Now it was Tom's turn to smile, but he controlled his tongue and kept silent. He said to himself that he would not say a word, even when his aunt came in, but would sit perfectly still till she asked who had broken the basin. Then he would tell, and it

---

[1] To glance=to give a quick look at.

would be delightful to see that model boy get a good beating. He was so wild with joy that he could hardly keep still when the old lady came back and stood above the broken pieces, looking angrily over her spectacles. He said to himself, " Now she's going to hit Sid." And the next instant he was flat on the floor ! Her palm was uplifted to strike again, when Tom cried out:

" Hi ! Why are you hitting me? Sid broke it ! "

Aunt Polly paused, puzzled, and Tom looked at her for healing pity. But when she had recovered from her surprise she only said:

" H'm ! Well, I'm sure you deserved it. No doubt you were in some mischief while I was in the kitchen."

Then her conscience pricked her, and she longed to say something kind and loving; but she judged that this would be taken as a confession that she had been in the wrong, and discipline forbade that. So she kept silent, and went about her housework with a troubled heart. Tom sat gloomily in a corner and nursed his sorrows. He knew, through tearful eyes, that she glanced tenderly at him now and again, asking for forgiveness; but he refused to take any notice. He imagined himself lying on his deathbed and his aunt bending over him, begging for one little forgiving word, but he would turn his face to the wall and die without saying that word. Ah, how would she feel then? And he imagined himself brought home from the river, dead, with his curls all wet, and his poor hands still for ever, and his broken heart at rest. She would throw herself upon him, and her tears would fall like rain. She would pray God to give her back her boy, and promise she would never, never ill-treat him any more. But he would lie there, cold and pale, and make no sign, poor little sufferer. He was so affected by these visions that he had to keep on swallowing. His eyes swam in tears, which overflowed and ran down from the end of his nose.

He was enjoying his sorrow so much that any cheer-

fulness was unwelcome. When his cousin Mary danced
in, delighted to be home again after a week's visit to
the country, he got up and moved in clouds and darkness out at one door as she brought song and sunshine
in at the other. His unhappy heart desired to be alone,
and so he wandered far away from the places where
boys usually met. A log raft[1] on the river invited him.
He sat down on its outer edge and gazed at the wide
river, wishing that he could be drowned at once, without suffering the usual pains.

Not long after, as Tom was undressing for bed, Sid
woke up. He said nothing. He knew from the expression on Tom's face that it would be unwise to ask him
any questions. Tom got into bed without saying his
prayers, and Sid made a note of this bad behaviour.

CHAPTER 4

TOM IS "ILL"

MONDAY morning found Tom Sawyer miserable. Monday morning always found him so, because it began
another week's slow suffering in school.

Tom lay in bed thinking. He wished that he was ill.
Then he could stay away from school. He thought that
he could detect signs of stomach-ache, and began to
encourage them with considerable hope, but they soon
grew faint, and died away. He considered further.
Suddenly he discovered something. One of his upper
teeth was loose. This was lucky. He was about to
groan when it occurred[2] to him that if he said so his
aunt would pull it out, and that would hurt. Then he
remembered hearing the doctor speak about a patient
who had spent two or three weeks in bed and who had

[1] A raft = large pieces of wood joined together to make a flat boat.

[2] To occur = to happen; it occurred to him = the thought came to him.

nearly lost a finger through blood-poisoning. So the boy eagerly drew his sore toe from under the sheet and held it up for inspection. Then he began groaning loudly.

But Sid slept on, unconscious.

Tom groaned louder, and fancied that he began to feel pain in the toe.

There was no result from Sid.

By this time Tom was breathing heavily with his efforts. He had a rest, and then swelled himself up and produced one admirable groan after another.

Sid slept on.

Tom was annoyed. He called, "Sid! Sid!" and shook him. This worked well, and Tom began to groan again. Sid yawned, stretched and then began to stare at Tom. Tom went on groaning.

"Tom! I say, Tom!" said Sid.

There was no reply.

"Here, Tom! Tom! What's the matter, Tom?" Sid shook him and looked in his face anxiously.

"Oh, don't, Sid. Don't shake me," Tom moaned.

"Why, what's the matter, Tom? I must call auntie."

"No, never mind. It'll be over soon, perhaps. Don't call anybody."

"But I must! Don't groan so, Tom; it's awful. How long have you been like this?"

"Hours. Ow! Oh, don't shake me, Sid. You'll kill me."

"Tom, why didn't you wake me sooner? Oh, Tom, don't. It makes me feel queer to hear you. What's the matter, Tom?"

"I forgive you everything, Sid. (Groan.) Everything you've ever done to me. When I'm dead——"

"Oh, Tom, you aren't dying, are you? Don't, Tom. Oh, don't. Perhaps——"

"I forgive everybody, Sid. (Groan.) Tell them so. And, Sid, give my window-frame and my cat with one eye to that new girl who has come to town, and tell her——"

But Sid had snatched up his clothes and gone. So well was Tom's imagination working that he was really suffering now. His groans had quite a genuine tone.

Sid flew downstairs.

"Oh, Aunt Polly, come! Tom's dying!" he cried. "Dying!"

"Yes. Don't wait. Come quickly!"

"Rubbish! I don't believe it."

But she rushed upstairs in spite of her disbelief, with Sid and Mary at her heels, and her face grew white, too, and her lips trembled. When she reached the bed she gasped out:

"Tom, what's the matter with you?"

"Oh, auntie, my——"

"What's the matter with you? What *is* the matter with you, child?"

"Oh, auntie, my big toe's *dead*!"

The old lady sank down into a chair, and laughed a little, then cried a little, then did both together. This helped her to recover, and she said:

"Tom, what a shock you did give me! Now stop that nonsense and get out of bed."

The groans ceased and the pain vanished from the toe. The boy felt a little foolish, and he said:

"Aunt Polly, it *did* seem to be dead, and it hurt so much that I did not feel the pain in my tooth at all."

"Your tooth? What's the matter with your tooth?"

"One of them is loose, and it aches awfully."

"There, there, don't begin that groaning again. Open your mouth. Well, your tooth *is* loose, but you're not going to die of that. Mary, get me a silk thread, and a red-hot coal from the kitchen."

"Please, auntie, don't pull it out. It doesn't hurt any more. Please, auntie, *I* don't want to stay away from school."

"Oh, you don't, don't you? So all this howling was because you thought you'd manage to stay away from school and go fishing? Tom, Tom, I love you so, and you seem to try every way you can to break my old heart with your tricks."

By this time the instruments were ready. The old lady made one end of the silk thread fast to Tom's tooth and tied the other to the bedpost. Then she seized the burning coal and suddenly thrust it almost in the boy's face. The tooth hung from the bedpost, now.

But all sufferings have their rewards. As Tom was going to school after breakfast, he was the envy of every boy he met, because the gap in his upper row of teeth enabled him to spit in a new and admirable way.

Soon afterwards Tom met the young outcast of the village, Huckleberry Finn, the son of the town drunkard. Huckleberry was hated and dreaded by all the mothers of the town because he was idle, lawless, ill-bred and bad, and because all their children admired him, delighted in his forbidden society and wished they dared to be like him. Like the rest of the respectable boys, Tom envied Huckleberry his gay life of freedom, and had been given strict orders not to play with him. So he played with him every time he got a chance. Huckleberry was always dressed like a scarecrow. He came and went of his own free will. He slept on doorsteps in fine weather, and in empty barrels in wet. He did not have to go to school or to church, or call anyone master, or obey anybody. He could go fishing or swimming when and where he chose, and stay as long as it suited him. Nobody forbade him to fight. He could sit up as late as he pleased. He was always the first boy to walk barefooted in the spring and the last to wear shoes again in the autumn. He never had to wash or put on clean clothes. He could swear wonderfully. In a word, that boy had everything that helps to make life delightful. So thought every respectable boy in St. Petersburg.

"Hello, Huckleberry! What's that you've got?" asked Tom.

"Hello! Dead cat."

"Let me see it, Huck. How stiff it is! What's a dead cat good for, Huck?"

"For curing warts."[1]

"But how do you cure them?"

"Why, you take the cat about midnight to a grave-yard, where somebody that was wicked has been buried. When it's midnight a devil will come, or per-haps two or three. But you can't see them; you can only hear something like the wind, or perhaps hear them talking. When they're taking that wicked fellow away, you throw your cat after them and say, ' Devil, follow body; cat, follow devil; warts, follow cat; I've finished with you.' That will cure *any* wart."

"It sounds all right. Have you ever tried it, Huck?"

"No, but old Mother Hopkins told me."

"Well, that's good enough, because they say she's a witch. Huck, when are you going to try the cat?"

"To-night. I believe they'll come after old Horse Williams to-night."

"But he was buried on Saturday, Huck. Didn't they get him on Saturday night?"

"Why, how you talk! How could their charms work before midnight? And then it's Sunday. Devils don't creep about much on a Sunday, as far as *I* know."

"I never thought of that. That's so. Will you let me go with you?"

"Of course—if you're not afraid."

"Afraid? Not likely. Will you meow like a cat?"

"Yes, and you meow back if you get a chance. The last time you kept me meowing outside the house till old Hays began throwing things at me and saying, ' Curse that cat!' So I threw a brick through his window; but don't tell."

"I won't. I couldn't meow that night because auntie

---

[1] A wart=a small hard growth on the skin.

was watching me, but I'll meow this time."

The boys separated. When Tom reached the little school he marched boldly in as if he had come as fast as he could. The teacher was nodding amidst the hum of study. The interruption roused him.

"Thomas Sawyer!"

Tom knew that when his name was pronounced in full, it meant trouble.

"Sir!"

"Come here. Now, why are you late again, as usual?"

Tom was about to lie, when he saw two long tails of yellow hair hanging down from a head that he recognized, and by that head was *the only vacant seat* on the girls' side of the school. He instantly said:

"*I stopped to talk with Huckleberry Finn!*"

The teacher stared at him as if he could not believe his ears. The hum of study ceased. The pupils wondered whether this boy had gone mad. The teacher said:

"You—you did what?"

"I stopped to talk with Huckleberry Finn."

The boy's words were quite distinct and could not be misunderstood.

"Tom Sawyer, this is the most astounding confession I have ever listened to. You deserve a severe punishment. Take off your coat."

The stick rose and fell until the teacher's arm was tired. Then the order followed:

"Now, sir, go and sit with the *girls*! And let this be a warning to you."

When all the pupils laughed, Tom seemed to look ashamed, but in reality that look was caused by his worship of the unknown angel and by his amazement at his luck. He sat down upon the end of the bench, and the girl proudly moved away from him. Tom sat still and seemed to study his book. Soon the other children ceased to pay any attention to him, and the accustomed school murmur rose upon the dull air once more. Presently the boy began to steal glances at the girl. She observed him, pulled a face at him, and turned the back of her head to him for a minute. When she cautiously looked round again, he was drawing something at the back of his book, hiding his work with his left hand. For some time the girl refused to notice, but at last she hesitatingly whispered:

" Let me see it."

Tom uncovered a weak drawing of a house with a corkscrew of smoke coming from the chimney. Then he added a man like a mast in the front yard. The girl said:

" I wish I could draw."

" It's easy," whispered Tom. " I'll teach you."

" Oh, will you? When?"

" At dinner-time."

" Good. That's a promise."

" What's your name?"

" Becky Thatcher. What's yours? Oh, I know. It's Thomas Sawyer."

" That's the name they use when they beat me. I'm Tom when I'm good. Call me Tom, will you?"

" Yes."

Just at this moment a finger and thumb closed on his ear and raised him to his feet. He was led across the schoolroom and set down in his own seat, amidst the laughter of the whole school. Then the teacher stood over him during a few awful moments, and finally moved away to his chair without saying a word. But although Tom's ear burned, his heart was singing.

CHAPTER 5

THE QUARREL: OUTLAWS

THE harder Tom tried to fasten his mind on his book, the more his ideas wandered. So at last, with a sigh and a yawn, he gave it up. It seemed to him that the noon interval would never come. The air was utterly dead. There was not a breath of air stirring. It was the sleepiest of sleepy days. Away in the flaming sunshine Cardiff Hill lifted its soft green sides through a veil of heat purple with distance. A few birds floated on lazy wings high in the air. No other living things were visible, except some cows, and they were asleep. Tom's heart ached to be free, or to have something of interest to do to pass the weary time.

At last the morning lessons ended, and Tom flew to Becky Thatcher. They sat together, with an exercise-book before them, and Tom gave Becky the pencil and held her hand in his, guiding it, and so created another surprising house. Tom was in heaven.

" Do you like rats? " he said.

" No, I hate them ! "

" Well, I do, too—live ones. But I mean dead ones, to swing around your head with a piece of string."

" No, I don't care for rats much. What *I* like is chewing-gum ! "[1]

" Oh, I wish I had some now ! "

" Do you? I've got some. We'll share it."

So Becky handed Tom his share, and they sat chewing happily.

" Have you ever been to a circus? " asked Tom.

" Yes, and my father's going to take me again some time if I'm good."

[1] Chewing gum=a kind of sweet; to chew=to break up with the teeth; gum=a sticky liquid obtained from trees.

"I've been to a circus three or four times—lots of times. I'm going to be a lion-tamer when I grow up!"

"Oh, are you? That will be nice. They look lovely dressed up in uniforms."

"Yes, that's so. And they get a lot of money, almost a dollar a day, Ben Rogers says. I say, Becky, please tell me that you won't have any friend but me, and that when we're coming to school or going home, you'll always walk with me; and I'll choose you at parties and you choose me."

"That sounds nice."

"Doesn't it? Why, Amy Lawrence and I——"

Becky's big eyes told Tom of his mistake, and he stopped confused.

"Oh, Tom! You like Amy Lawrence more than me."

The child began to cry. Tom said:

"Don't cry, Becky. I don't care for her any more."

"Yes you do, Tom. You know you do."

Tom tried to comfort her, but she pushed him away and went on crying. Tom stood about, restless and uneasy. Then he said hesitatingly:

"Becky, I—I don't care for anybody but you."

She did not reply.

"Becky, won't you say something?"

Becky's tears continued to flow.

Tom got out his chief jewel, the brass door-handle, and held it out so that she could see it.

"Please, Becky, won't you take it?"

She struck it to the floor. Then Tom marched off and over the hills and far away, to return to school no more that day.

Half an hour later Tom was disappearing behind Widow Douglas's house on the top of Cardiff Hill, and the school was hardly visible far away in the valley below him. He entered a thick wood, picked his way to the centre of it, and sat down under a spreading oak tree. He sat for a long time with his elbows on his knees and his chin in his hands. It seemed to him that life was full of trouble. He remembered a school friend who had died recently. It must be very peaceful, he thought, to lie and sleep and dream for ever and ever, with the wind whispering through the trees and over the grass and flowers of the grave, and nothing to grieve about any more. If he only had a good Sunday-school record he might be willing to go. Now as to this girl; he had been very nice to her, and had been treated like a dog. She would be sorry some day, perhaps when it was too late. Ah, if he could die just for a short time!

Just then the sound of a toy tin horn came faintly through the forest. Tom threw off his coat, raked away some dead branches from behind a rotten log, revealing a bow and arrow, a wooden sword and a tin horn, and in a moment had seized these things and leapt away. He soon stopped under a great tree, blew an answering note, and began to tiptoe and look cautiously out, this way and that. He said softly, to an imaginary company:

"Keep still, my merry men! Keep hidden till I blow."

Joe Harper now appeared, dressed and armed as Tom.

"Stop!" called Tom. "Who comes here into Sherwood Forest without my permission?"

"I, a knight, need no man's permission. What villain——"

"—dares address me with such insolence," said Tom, reminding him, for they were using the words of one of their favourite books, *The Adventures of Robin Hood.*

"What villain dares address me with such insolence?"

"I, Robin Hood, as your proud body soon shall

know."

"That famous outlaw? Gladly will I fight you. Guard yourself!"

They drew their swords, faced each other, foot to foot, with swords crossed, and began a stern, careful fight. Presently Tom said:

"Now you know how to do it. Let us fight faster."

So they fought faster, breathing heavily and sweating with the work. Soon Tom shouted:

"Fall! Fall! Why don't you fall?"

"I won't. Why don't you fall yourself? You're getting the worst of it."

"Why, that's nothing! *I* can't fall. It's not like that in the book. The book says, 'Then with one backhanded blow he killed the proud knight.' You have to turn round and let me hit you in the back."

It was impossible to contradict the book, so Joe turned, received the blow, and fell.

"Now," said Joe, getting up, "you've got to let me kill you. That's fair."

"Why, I can't do that. It's not in the book."

"Well, I call that very unfair."

"Well, Joe, I'll be the Sheriff of Nottingham, and you be Robin Hood a little while and kill me."

This was satisfactory, and so these scenes were acted. Then Tom became Robin Hood again, and lay dying, the blood flowing from his neglected wound. And at last Joe, representing a whole tribe of weeping outlaws, dragged him sadly out and put the bow into his weak hands. Tom said, "Where this arrow falls, there bury poor Robin Hood." Then he shot the arrow, and fell back, and would have died; but he landed on some thorns, and sprang up too gaily for a dead body.

The boys dressed themselves, hid their weapons, and went off grieving that there were no outlaws any more. They said that they would rather be outlaws for a year in Sherwood Forest than President of the United States for ever.

CHAPTER 6

IN THE GRAVEYARD

AT half-past nine that night Tom and Sid were sent to bed as usual. They said their prayers, and Sid was soon asleep. Tom lay awake and waited in restless impatience. The clock struck eleven. Then there came Huck's signal, the meowing of a cat. A minute later Tom was dressed and out of the window. He crept along the roof of the woodshed and then jumped to the ground. Huckleberry Finn was there, with his dead cat. The boys moved off and disappeared in the darkness.

Half an hour later they were stepping through the tall grass of the graveyard. It was on a hill, about a mile and a half from the village. A faint wind moaned through the trees, and Tom feared that it might be the spirits of the dead complaining about this disturbance of their rest. The boys talked in whispers, for the time and the place, the solemnity and the silence, had a depressing effect on them. They found the heap of newly dug earth which they were seeking, and crept within the protection of three great trees that grew within a few feet of the grave.

Then they waited in silence for what seemed a long time. The mournful cry of a distant bird was the only sound that troubled the dead stillness.

"Huck, do you believe the dead people like us to be here?" said Tom in a whisper.

"I wish I knew," whispered Huck. "It's awfully solemn, isn't it?"

"It is."

There was a long pause.

"I say, Huck, do you think Horse Williams can hear us talking?"

"Of course he can. At least his spirit can."

Another long pause followed.

"I wish I'd said *Mister* Williams," breathed Tom. "But I never meant any harm. Everybody calls him Horse."

"You should be very careful how you talk about these dead people, Tom."

This was discouraging, and conversation died again. Suddenly Tom seized Huck's arm and exclaimed:

"*Sh!*"

"What is it, Tom?"

The two boys held on to each other, their hearts beating fast.

"*Sh!* There it is again! Didn't you hear it?"

"Oh, Tom, they're coming! They're coming! What'll we do?"

"I don't know. Do you think they'll see us?"

"Oh, Tom, they can see in the dark just like cats. I wish I hadn't come."

The boys bent their heads together and scarcely breathed. A dull sound of voices floated up from the far end of the graveyard.

"Look there!" whispered Tom. "What is it?"

"It's devil-fire! Oh, Tom, this is awful!"

Some vague figures approached through the gloom, swinging an old-fashioned lamp.

"It's the devils, I'm sure. Three of them. Tom, we'll never get away alive. Can you pray?"

"I'll try, but don't be afraid. They're not going to hurt us."

"*Sh!*"

"What is it, Huck?"

"They're *human beings*! One of them is, I'm certain. That's old Potter's voice."

"No, it isn't, is it?"

"I know it. Don't stir. He isn't sharp enough to

notice us. Drunk as usual, I expect."

"All right, I'll keep still. Here they come again. I say, Huck, I know another of them. It's Redskin Joe!"

"That's so. That murdering half-breed. I'd rather have devils! What do they want?"

The three men reached the grave, and stood within a few feet of the boys' hiding-place.

"Here it is," said the third voice, and the owner of it held the lamp up and revealed the face of young Dr. Robinson.

Potter and Redskin Joe had a handcart, from which they took a blanket,[1] a rope and two spades. Then they began to open the grave.

"Hurry, men," said the doctor in a low voice. "The moon may come out at any moment."

They made an indistinct reply and went on digging. For some time there was no noise but the sound of the spades moving the earth. Finally a spade struck the coffin, and within another minute or two the men had lifted it out. They broke off the lid with their spades, got out the body and dropped it roughly on the ground. The moon sailed out from behind the clouds and lit up the chalky face. The handcart was got ready and the body was placed on it, covered with the blanket, and bound in its place with the rope. Potter took out a knife, cut the end of the rope, and then said:

"Now the cursed thing's ready, Sawbones, and you'll hand out another five dollars, or here it stays."

"That's the way to talk," said Redskin Joe.

"What does this mean?" asked the doctor. "You demanded your pay in advance, and I've paid you."

"Yes, and you've done more than that," said Redskin Joe, approaching the doctor. "Five years ago you drove me away from your father's kitchen one

---

[1] A blanket=a thick woollen cloth used as a bed covering.

night when I came to ask for a bit of bread, and you called me a scoundrel. When I swore that I'd make you suffer for that, even if it took me a hundred years, your father had me put in prison as a vagabond. Did you think that I, with native blood in me, would forget such treatment? And now I've got you, and you must pay for it."

He was threatening the doctor with his fist in his face by this time. The doctor struck out suddenly and knocked the villain down. Potter dropped his knife and exclaimed, "Here, don't strike my partner!" The next moment Potter and the doctor were fighting fiercely. Redskin Joe sprang to his feet, his eyes flaming with fury, snatched up Potter's knife, and went creeping, cat-like, about the struggling men, seeking for an opportunity. Suddenly the doctor tore himself free, seized the heavy headboard of Williams's grave and stunned Potter with it. At the same instant the half-breed saw his chance and drove the knife up to the handle in the young man's breast. He staggered and fell partly upon Potter, flooding him with his blood. At the same moment the clouds covered up the dreadful spectacle, and the two terrified boys seized this opportunity to creep away in the darkness.

When the moon came out again, Redskin Joe was standing over the two men, regarding them thoughtfully. The doctor murmured something, gave a long gasp or two, and was still. The half-breed muttered, "That account is settled, curse you." Then he robbed the body. After doing so, he put the fatal knife in Potter's right hand, and sat down on the broken coffin. Three—four—five minutes passed, and then Potter began to stir and moan. His hand closed upon the knife. He raised it, glanced at it and let it fall with a shiver. Then he sat up, pushing the body from him, and gazed at it and around him confusedly. His eyes met Redskin Joe's.

"Good heavens! What's this, Joe?" he said.

"It's a nasty business," replied Redskin Joe, without moving. "What did you do it for?"

"*I!* *I* didn't do it."

Potter trembled and went white.

"I thought I wasn't drunk. I shouldn't have touched any drink to-night. But it's in my head yet. I can't remember anything about this. Tell me, Joe—truthfully, now, old fellow—did I do it, Joe? Upon my soul and honour I swear that I never meant to, Joe. Tell me how it happened, Joe. Oh, it's awful! And he was such a fine young doctor."

"Why, you two were struggling, and he hit you with the headboard and knocked you down. Then you got up, snatched the knife and stuck it into him just as he hit you again, and you've been lying here till now."

"Oh, I didn't know what I was doing! It was all on account of the drink and excitement, I'm sure. I never used a weapon in my life before, Joe." The poor creature dropped on his knees and held out his arms before the murderer. "Joe, don't tell! Say that you won't tell, Joe, that's a good fellow. I've always liked you, Joe, and defended you, too. You won't tell, will you, Joe?"

"No, you've always been good to me, Potter, and I'll keep my mouth shut."

"Oh, Joe, you're an angel! I'll bless you for this till my dying day." He began to cry.

"Come, now, that's enough of that," said Redskin Joe. "You go that way and I'll go this. Move, now, and don't leave any tracks behind you."

Potter hurried away and the half-breed stood looking after him. "If he's as much stunned with the blow and as stupid with the drink as he seems to be," Redskin Joe muttered, "he won't think of the knife till he's gone so far that he'll be afraid to come back for it, the coward."

CHAPTER 7

TOM AND HUCK SWEAR AN OATH

THE two boys flew on and on towards the village, speechless with horror. They glanced backwards over their shoulders from time to time, as if they feared that they might be followed.

"If we can only get to the old mill before we break down," gasped Tom. "I can't bear this much longer."

Huckleberry's heavy breathing was his only reply. At last they burst through the open door of the old mill and fell, grateful and exhausted, in the sheltering shadows. After a time their breathing became regular, and Tom said:

"Huck, what do you think will happen?"

"If Dr. Robinson dies, Redskin Joe will be hanged."

Tom thought for a moment, and then said:

"Who'll tell? We?"

"What are you talking about? If we do, and Redskin Joe isn't hanged, why, he'll kill us some time or other, as sure as we're lying here. If anybody tells, let Potter do it, if he's foolish enough. He's generally drunk enough."

Tom went on thinking, and then asked:

"Huck, how can Potter tell? He doesn't know anything about it."

"Why doesn't he know?"

"Potter couldn't see anything. He'd just been stunned when Redskin Joe struck the doctor with his knife."

"That's so, Tom."

After another thoughtful silence, Tom asked:

"Huck, are you sure that you can keep quiet about it?"

"Tom, we *must*. You know that. If we tell people

what we have seen, and if that devilish half-breed escapes hanging, he'll drown us just as if we were a couple of cats. Now, Tom, we must swear to each other to keep our mouths shut."

"I agree, Huck. It's the best thing. Shall we just hold hands and swear that we——"

"Oh, no, that wouldn't do for this. That's good enough for ordinary things, but there ought to be writing about a big thing like this. And blood."

Tom highly approved of this idea. It was deep, and dark, and awful; the hour, the circumstances and the surroundings suited it. He picked up a clean, flat piece of wood that lay in the moonlight, took the end of a pencil out of his pocket, got the moonlight on his work, and, with his tongue between his teeth, wrote these lines:

Huck Finn and Tom Sawyer swear that they will keep their mouths shut about this and they wish that they may drop dead in their tracks if they ever tell.

Huckleberry was filled with admiration of the ease with which Tom wrote and of the superior style of his language.

Then Tom unwound the thread from one of his needles, and each boy pricked his thumb and pressed out a drop of blood. In time, by pressing over and over again, Tom managed to sign the letters T and S, using the end of his little finger for a pen. Then he showed Huckleberry how to make an H and an F, and the oath was complete. They buried the piece of wood close to the wall with some mournful ceremonies and charms, and the chains that bound their tongues were considered to be locked and the key thrown away.

Then they separated.

When Tom crept in at the bedroom window, the night was almost ended. He undressed with excessive caution, and fell asleep congratulating himself that nobody knew of his absence. He was not aware that Sid had been awake for an hour.

When Tom awoke, Sid had dressed and gone. There was a late look in the light. He was startled. Why had he not been called? In a few minutes he was downstairs, feeling stiff and sleepy. The family were still at the table, but they had finished breakfast. His aunt did not blame him, but sat with downcast eyes. Tom had his breakfast in gloomy silence.

After breakfast his aunt took him aside, wept over him and asked him how he could break her old heart so by his bad behaviour. She told him that she had given up hope of making him a good boy. This was worse than a thousand whippings, and Tom's heart was sorer now than his body. He cried, begged for forgiveness, and promised over and over again not to misbehave. When he was finally dismissed, he felt that she had little confidence in his promises and that she had not forgiven him entirely.

He felt too miserable to take his revenge against Sid, so Sid's speedy retreat through the back gate was unnecessary. At school, while he was being punished with Joe Harper for staying away the day before, he looked as if he did not care what happened to him. He sat down, rested his elbows on his desk and his jaws in his hands, and stared at the wall with the stony stare of suffering that has reached the limit and can go no farther. His elbow was pressing against some hard substance. After a long time he slowly and sadly changed his position, and took up this object with a sigh. It was wrapped in paper. He unwrapped it. A sigh from the very depths followed, and his heart broke. It was his brass door-handle! This last straw broke the camel's back.

CHAPTER 8

POTTER IS ARRESTED

JUST before midday the whole village was electrified by the shocking news. It was reported that a bloody knife had been found close to the murdered man. Somebody had recognized it and stated that it belonged to Potter. It was said that a villager, delayed on his way home, had come across Potter washing himself in a stream about one o'clock in the morning, and that Potter had at once crept off. These were suspicious circumstances, especially the washing, which was not a habit with Potter. Horsemen had gone in search down all the roads in every direction, and the Sheriff was confident that he would be captured before night.

Of course the pupils were given a holiday that afternoon. All the villagers were flocking to the graveyard. Tom's heartbreak vanished, and he joined the procession. The dreadful place drew him like a magnet in spite of himself. There somebody pinched his arm. He turned, and his eyes met Huckleberry's.

"Poor young fellow!". "This ought to be a lesson to grave-robbers!" "Potter will hang for this if they catch him!" These were the general remarks.

Now Tom shivered from head to heel, for he caught sight of the stern face of Redskin Joe. At this moment the crowd began to hurry forward, and voices shouted, "It's Potter! He's coming himself! Look out! He's turning! Don't let him get away!"

People in the branches of the trees over Tom's head said that he was not trying to get away, but that he only looked doubtful and lost.

The crowd fell apart now, and the Sheriff came through leading Potter by the arm. The poor fellow's face was as white as a sheet, and his eyes showed the fear that was in his heart. When he stood before the murdered man, he put his face in his hands and burst into tears.

"I didn't do it, friends," he moaned; "I swear I didn't do it."

"Who accused you?" shouted a voice.

Potter raised his head and looked around him with a terrible hopelessness in his eyes. He saw Redskin Joe and exclaimed, "Oh, Joe, you promised me that you'd never——"

"Is that your knife?" asked the Sheriff, thrusting it before him.

Potter would have fallen if they had not caught him. He murmured, "Tell them, Joe; tell them. It's no use."

Then Huckleberry and Tom stood dumb and staring, and heard the stony-hearted liar make his statement. They expected every moment that the clear sky would deliver God's lightnings upon his head, and wondered to see how long the punishment was delayed. When he had finished and still stood alive and whole, their weak intention to break their oath and save the poor, betrayed prisoner's life faded and vanished. It was plain that this villain was under the protection of the Devil, and it would be fatal to interfere with the agent of such an awful power as that. He had now become the most horribly interesting person they had ever looked upon, and they could not take their eyes off his face. They inwardly resolved to watch him at night when they had an opportunity, in the hope of catching sight of his dreadful master.

Tom's fearful secret and troubled conscience disturbed his sleep for a week after this, and at breakfast one morning Sid said, "Tom, you talk in your sleep so much that you keep me awake half the night."

Tom paled and dropped his eyes.

"It's a bad sign," said Aunt Polly. "What is worrying you, Tom?"

"Nothing; nothing that I know of." But the boy's hand shook so much that he spilled his coffee.

"And you do talk such queer nonsense," Sid continued. "Last night you said, 'It's blood, it's blood, that's what it is!' You said that over and over again."

Aunt Polly came to Tom's relief without knowing it.

"It's that dreadful murder," she said. "I dream about it almost every night myself. Sometimes I dream that I did it."

Every day or two during this time of sorrow Tom went to the prison, a little brick building at the edge of the village. When he had a chance, he slipped small comforts such as tobacco and matches through the barred window to the "murderer." These gifts greatly helped to ease Tom's conscience. The villagers had a strong desire to whip Redskin Joe for body-snatching, but he was regarded as such a dangerous scoundrel that nobody was willing to take the lead in the matter, and so it was given up.

CHAPTER 9

MEDICINE

A NEW and weighty matter occupied Tom's mind. Becky Thatcher had stopped coming to school. Tom had struggled with his pride for a few days, and tried to forget her, but failed. He heard that she was ill. If she should die! He no longer took an interest in swimming, or even in Sherwood Forest. He went about looking very depressed. His aunt was worried, and began to try all sorts of medicines on him. She bought all the "Health" papers regularly, and believed all the solemn nonsense which they contained. The water treatment was new now, and Tom's low condition was an unexpected piece of good fortune to her. She took him out at daylight every morning, stood him up in the woodshed, and drowned him with a flood of cold water. Then she rubbed him down with a towel like sandpaper, and so made him recover. Then she rolled him up in a wet sheet and put him away under blankets till she sweated his soul clean and "the yellow stains of it came through the skin," as Tom said. Yet in spite of all this the boy remained as sad as a funeral.

Aunt Polly decided that this depression must be broken up at any cost. Now she heard of Pain-killer for the first time. She ordered a dozen bottles at once. She tasted it and was filled with gratitude. It was simply fire in liquid form. She gave Tom a teaspoonful and watched with the deepest anxiety for the result. A wild look came into Tom's eye, he gave a deep gasp and then started to race around the room. Aunt Polly was delighted. Her troubles were over, for the depression was broken up.

Tom felt that it was time to wake up and protect himself. So he thought over various plans of relief, and finally decided to pretend to be fond of Pain-killer. He asked for it so often that he became a nuisance. His aunt ended by telling him to help himself and stop worrying her; but she watched the bottle secretly. She found that the medicine did really disappear, but it did not occur to her that the boy was curing a crack in the sitting-room floor with it.

One day Tom was giving medical attention to the crack when his aunt's yellow cat, Peter, came along, singing, eyeing the spoon greedily, and begging for a taste.

"Don't ask for it unless you want it, Peter," said Tom.

But Peter showed that he did want it.

"Are you sure?"

Peter was sure.

" Now you've asked for it, and I'll give it to you, because I'm not selfish, but if you find you don't like it, you mustn't blame anybody but yourself."

Peter still seemed eager, so Tom forced his mouth open and poured down the Pain-killer. Peter sprang a couple of yards into the air, shouted a war-cry and then flew round and round the room, banging against the furniture, upsetting the flower-pots, and causing general destruction. Next lie rose on his back legs and danced madly around, screaming with joy. Then he went rushing round the house again, spreading more destruction in his path. Aunt Polly entered in time to see him take some astounding leaps into the air, give a final piercing scream, and sail through the open window, carrying the rest of the flower-pots with him. The old lady stood rooted to the floor with astonishment, peering over her glasses. Tom lay on the floor, splitting his sides with laughter.

" Tom, what on earth is wrong with that cat?"

" *I* don't know, aunt," gasped the boy.

" Why, I've never seen anything like it. What *did* make him behave like that?"

" Indeed I don't know, Aunt Polly. Cats always do that when they're enjoying themselves."

" They do, do they?" There was something in her tone that made Tom expect trouble.

The old lady bent down. The handle of the teaspoon was visible under the rug. She took it and held it up. Tom looked guilty. She raised him by the usual handle —his ear—and slapped him.

" Now, why did you treat that poor, dumb creature like that?"

" I was pretending to be his aunt."

" What do you mean?"

" I was pretending to be his aunt and trying to burn the bowels out of him."

This was putting the matter in a new light. What

was cruel to a cat might be cruel to a boy too. She began to soften; she felt sorry. Her eyes watered a little, and she put her hand on Tom's head and said gently:

"I didn't mean to be cruel, Tom. And, Tom, the medicine did do you good."

"It did *him* good, too. The way he flew round the room——"

"Oh, run away, before you make me lose my temper again. Try to be a good boy for once, and then you needn't take any more medicine."

Tom reached school early. It was noticed that this strange thing had been occurring every day recently. He waited beside the gate instead of playing with his friends. When Jeff Thatcher arrived, Tom spoke to him and tried in a roundabout way to get some information about Becky, but the stupid boy could not understand what Tom wanted. Tom watched and watched, hoping when a dress came in sight, and hating the owner of it as soon as he saw that she was not the right one. Then one more dress passed in at the gate, and Tom's heart gave a great leap. The next instant he was shouting, laughing, chasing boys, standing on his head, jumping over the fence at the risk of life and limb, doing all the heroic[1] deeds he could think of, and keeping an eye on Becky Thatcher, to see if she was noticing. She never looked. He broke through a group of boys, scattering them in every direction, and fell beside Becky, almost upsetting her. She turned away, with her nose in the air.

"H'm! Some people think they're very smart," he heard her say mockingly.

Tom's cheeks burned. He rose to his feet and walked away, crushed.

[1] A hero = a man admired for his noble qualities, such as bravery; heroic = very brave.

CHAPTER 10

PIRATES

TOM'S mind was made up now. He was gloomy and desperate. He was a lonely, friendless boy, he thought. When they found out what they had driven him to, perhaps they would be sorry. Nothing would please them but to get rid of him; let it be so, and let them blame him for the result. Yes, they had forced him to it at last. He would lead a life of crime. There was no choice.

By this time he was far away from school, and the bell for lessons came faintly to his ear. The tears came into his eyes as he thought that he would never, never hear that old familiar sound again.

Just at this point he met his best friend, Joe Harper, who had evidently a great and mournful purpose in his heart. Tom, wiping his eyes with his sleeve, began to moan something about his determination to escape from lack of sympathy at home by wandering into the great world, never to return. He ended by hoping that Joe would not forget him.

But it appeared that Joe had also made up his mind to run away from home. He had been searching for Tom to give him this important piece of information. His mother had whipped him for drinking some cream which he had not tasted and which he knew nothing about. It was plain that she was tired of him and wished him to go.

As the two boys walked sorrowing along, they swore to stand by each other and to be brothers till death relieved them of their troubles. Then they began to lay their plans. Joe wanted to be a holy man and live on bits of bread in a cave, and die, at last, of cold, want and grief; but after listening to Tom, he agreed that there were some outstanding advantages about a life of crime, and so he consented to be a pirate.

Three miles below St. Petersburg, at a point where the Mississippi River was about a mile wide, there was a long, narrow, wooded island, with a shallow sand-bar at the head of it. This island would be a suitable meeting-place. It was not inhabited, and lay far over towards the farther bank, facing a thick forest. So Jackson's Island was chosen. Then they searched for Huckleberry Finn, and he joined them directly, for all professions were the same to him.

They arranged to meet at a lonely spot on the river bank two miles above the village at their favourite hour, midnight. There was a small log raft there which they intended to capture. Each would bring hooks and fishing-lines, and such food as he could steal in the dark and mysterious way of a true pirate. During the afternoon they told everyone that soon the town would " hear something startling." All who got this vague news were warned to " keep it a secret and wait."

About midnight Tom arrived with some meat and a few trifles, and stopped in the thick bushes on a steep slope overlooking the meeting-place. He gave a low whistle. It was answered from the foot of the slope. Tom whistled twice more. These signals were answered in the same way.

" Who goes there? " said a fierce voice.

" Tom Sawyer, the Black Avenger of the Spanish Seas. Give me your names."

" Huck Finn the Red-handed and Joe Harper the Terror of the Oceans." Tom had provided these titles from his favourite literature.

" Give the pass-word."

Two whispers delivered the same awful word at the same time to the breathless night:

"BLOOD!"

Then Tom rolled his meat down the slope and let himself down after it, tearing both skin and clothes in the effort. There was an easy, comfortable path along the bank at the foot of the slope, but Tom knew that a real pirate preferred difficulty and danger to ease and comfort.

The Terror of the Oceans had brought a big bag full of loaves and had tired himself out carrying it there. Finn the Red-handed had stolen a frying-pan[1] and a quantity of tobacco. The Black Avenger of the Spanish Seas said that they could not start without some fire. That was a wise thought, for matches were hardly known there in those days. They saw a fire upon a great raft a hundred yards above, and they went and helped themselves to a glowing piece of wood. They made an exciting adventure of it, saying " *Sh!* " every now and then, suddenly stopping with finger on lip, moving with hands on imaginary knives and giving orders in fierce whispers. They knew that the raftsmen were all down at the village, but that did not matter; they had to steal the fire in the right piratical way.

They pushed off presently, Tom in command, Huck at the after oar and Joe at the forward. Tom, with a gloomy face and folded arms, gave his orders in a low, stern whisper.

" Bring her to the wind! "

" Aye, aye, sir! "

" Steady, stead-y-y-y! "

" Steady it is, sir! "

" What sails is she carrying? "

" Mainsails, sir! "

" Send the topsails up! Lively, now! "

" Aye, aye, sir! "

As the boys steadily and uneventfully drove the raft towards mid-river, it was no doubt understood that these orders were given only for " style," and were not

To fry = to cook in oil or fat.

intended to mean anything in particular.

Hardly a word was said during the next three-quarters of an hour. Now the raft was passing the few glimmering lights of the distant village. The Black Avenger stood still with folded arms, taking a last look at the scene of his former joys and later sufferings. He wished that those whom he had left for ever could see him now, on the stormy sea, facing hardships and death with a courageous heart. The other pirates were taking a last look, too. They looked so long that they nearly floated past the island. But they discovered the danger in time, and at about two o'clock in the morning the raft stuck on the sand-bar. They walked backwards and forwards through the shallow water until they had landed their supplies. They had found an old sail on the little raft, and this they spread over some bushes as a tent to shelter their food. They themselves would sleep in the open air in fine weather, as pirates should.

They built a fire in the wood, cooked some meat in the frying-pan and had it for supper with some of the loaves. It seemed glorious fun to be feasting in that wild, free way, far from civilization. The fire lit up their faces and the tree-trunks around. After supper, they stretched themselves out on the grass, filled with contentment.

" Isn't it jolly? " said Joe.

" It's *grand*," said Tom.

" I don't want anything better than this," said Huckleberry. " I don't get enough to eat usually, and here people can't come and kick and worry me."

Huckleberry now filled his pipe with tobacco, pressed a glowing coal to it, and blew out a cloud of sweet-smelling smoke. The other pirates envied him this impressive vice, and secretly determined to adopt it soon.

" What do pirates do? " asked Huck.

" Oh, they have a fine time," said Tom. " They

take ships and burn them, and get the money and bury it in awful places in their island where there are ghosts to watch it, and kill everybody in the ships."

" And they wear the loveliest clothes ! All gold and silver and diamonds," said Joe.

" I don't think I'm properly dressed for a pirate," said Huck, regarding his own clothes sadly, " but these are the only ones I've got."

But the other boys told him that the fine clothes would come fast enough after they had begun their adventures.

Gradually their talk died out and sleepiness began to steal upon the eyelids of the adventurers. The pipe dropped from the fingers of the Red-handed. The Terror of the Oceans and the Black Avenger had more difficulty in getting to sleep. They said their prayers silently and lying down, since there was nobody there with authority to make them kneel and say them aloud. As they were about to fall asleep, an unwelcome visitor crept up and could not be driven away. It was conscience. They began to feel a vague fear that it was wrong to run away from home. Next they thought of the stolen meat and bread. They tried to argue it away by reminding conscience that they had taken sweets and cakes and apples without permission dozens of times; but conscience would not accept such a thin argument. In the end, they were forced to admit that running off with cakes was only " taking," while running off with meat and loaves of bread was plain, simple stealing, and there was a command against that in the Bible. So in their hearts they resolved that as long as they were pirates they would have nothing to do with the crime of stealing. Conscience was satisfied, and these odd pirates fell peacefully asleep.

CHAPTER 11

ON THE ISLAND

WHEN Tom awoke in the morning, he wondered where he was. He sat up and rubbed his eyes and looked around. Then he remembered. It was the cool, grey dawn, and there was a delightful sense of peace in the deep calm and silence of the woods. Not a leaf stirred. Dewdrops stood upon the leaves and grass. A white layer of ashes covered the fire, and a blue thread of smoke rose straight into the air. Joe and Huck still slept.

Now, far away in the woods, a bird called. Another answered. Gradually the cool, dim grey of the morning whitened, and as gradually sounds multiplied and life revealed itself. The marvel of Nature shaking off sleep and going to work unfolded itself to the boy. A little green worm came crawling over a dewy leaf. Tom sat as still as a stone, with his hopes rising and falling as the creature still came towards him or showed a tendency to go elsewhere. When it finally came down upon Tom's leg and began a journey over him, his whole heart was glad, for that meant that he was going to have a new suit of clothes, without a shadow of doubt a glorious piratical uniform. Now a procession of ants appeared and went about their labours. One struggled with a dead spider five times as big as itself, and dragged it straight up a tree trunk. A tiny spotted beetle climbed up the great height of a grass-blade, and Tom bent down close to it and said:

" Ladybird, ladybird, fly away home,
  Your house is on fire, your children alone."

She flew off to see about it, which did not surprise the

42

boy, for he had long known that the ladybird was always ready to believe stories about fires.

The birds were singing madly by now. One swept down, a flash of blue flame, and stopped on a branch almost within the boy's reach. It leaned its head to one side and eyed the strangers with immense curiosity. All Nature was wide awake, long beams of sunlight pierced down through the leafy branches, and a few butterflies came dancing upon the scene.

Tom roused the other pirates, and in a minute or two they were chasing after and falling over each other in the shallow water of the sand-bar. The current had carried off their raft, but this only delighted them, since its going was something like burning the bridge between them and civilization.

They came back to camp wonderfully refreshed and as hungry as wolves. They soon had the camp-fire blazing up again. Huck found a spring of clear cold water close by and the boys made cups of leaves. Tom and Huck stepped to a promising place on the river bank and threw in their fishing-lines. Almost immediately they had their reward, enough fish for a family. They fried the fish and were astonished, for no fish had ever seemed so delicious before. They did not know that the quicker a fresh-water fish is on the fire after it is caught, the better it is; and they did not stop to think that sleeping, exercise and bathing in the open air had given them an excellent appetite.

They lay about in the shade after breakfast, while Huck had a smoke, and then went off through the woods exploring. They found plenty of things to be delighted with, but nothing to be astonished at. They had a swim every hour, so it was about the middle of the afternoon when they got back to camp. They were too hungry to stop to fish, but they had a good meal of meat, and threw themselves down in the shade to talk. But the talk soon began to drag, and then died. The quietness that hung over the woods, and the sense of loneliness, began to have an effect on the spirits of the boys. A vague longing crept upon them. This took dim shape presently. It was budding homesickness. Even Finn the Red-handed was dreaming of his doorsteps and his empty barrels. But they were all ashamed of their weakness and none was brave enough to say what was in his mind.

For some time now the boys had heard a peculiar sound in the distance. On hearing a louder sound, the boys started, glanced at each other inquiringly, and listened. There was a long silence, deep and unbroken. Then a dull sound came floating down out of the distance.

"What is it?" asked Joe in a whisper.

"Let's go and see," said Tom.

They sprang to their feet and hurried to the bank facing the village. They parted the bushes and peered out. The little steam ferryboat was not transporting people from bank to bank as usual, but was about a mile below the village. Her deck seemed crowded with people. There were many small boats being rowed about or floating with the current in the neighbourhood of the ferryboat, but the boys could not see what the men in them were doing. After a time there was a puff of white smoke from the side of the ferryboat, and as it rose in a lazy cloud that same dull sound was borne to the listeners again.

"I know now!" exclaimed Tom. "Somebody's drowned!"

"That's it," said Huck. "They did that last summer when Bill Turner was drowned. They shoot a big gun over the water, and that makes the body come up to the surface."

The boys continued to listen and watch. Then a revealing thought flashed through Tom's mind, and he exclaimed:

"Boys, I know who are drowned! We are!"

They felt like heroes in an instant. They were

missed; they were being wept over; hearts were break-
ing for them; and best of all, they were the talk of the
whole town, and the envy of all the boys. This was
glorious. It was worth while being a pirate, after all.

As twilight drew on, the ferryboat went back to her
accustomed business and the rowing-boats disappeared.
The pirates returned to camp. They were swollen with
vanity over their new importance and the great trouble
that they were causing. They caught fish, cooked
supper and ate it, and then began to guess what the
village was thinking and saying about them. But when
the shadows of night closed round them, they gradually
ceased to talk, and sat gazing into the fire, with their
minds evidently wandering elsewhere. The excitement
had gone, now, and Tom and Joe could not keep out
thoughts of certain persons at home who were not
enjoying their fine adventure as much as they were. A
sigh or two escaped unawares.

"Tom," said Joe hesitatingly, "pirates do go home
sometimes, don't they?"

Tom poured scorn upon him. Huck had not said a
word on the subject and was therefore free to join in
with Tom. Joe made excuses and firmly denied that he
was suffering from homesickness or that he wished to
desert.

As the night deepened, Huck began to nod, and
presently fell asleep. Joe followed next. Tom lay
watching the two for some time. At last he got up
cautiously and went searching among the grass in the
dim light of the camp-fire. He picked up and inspected
several large pieces of the thin white bark[1] of a tree, and
finally chose two. Then he knelt by the fire and wrote
something on each of these in pencil. One he rolled up
and put in his coat pocket, and the other he put in
Joe's cap, together with certain invaluable schoolboy
treasures, among them a piece of chalk, a rubber ball,
three fish-hooks and a special kind of marble. Then he
tiptoed away.

[1] Bark = the skin on the outside of a tree.

CHAPTER 12

WHAT TOM OVERHEARD

A FEW minutes later Tom was in the shallow water of the sand-bar, stepping towards the Illinois bank. Before the water reached his waist, he was half-way over. Then he began confidently to swim the remaining hundred yards. He reached the bank, pulled himself out and set out in his streaming garments through the woods. A little before ten o'clock he came out into an open space opposite the village, and saw the ferry-boat lying by the high bank. He crept down, slipped into the water, swam a few yards and climbed into the rowing-boat fastened to the ferryboat. He lay down and waited. Soon the bell rang, a voice gave the order to cast off, and the voyage began. Tom was pleased at his success, for he knew that it was the boat's last trip for the night. A quarter of an hour later the engine stopped. Tom slipped overboard and swam ashore, landing fifty yards downstream, where there was less danger of being seen. He flew along deserted lanes and soon found himself at his aunt's back fence. He climbed over and approached the window of Aunt Polly's room, for a light was burning there. There sat Aunt Polly, Sid, Mary and Joe Harper's mother, grouped together, talking. They were by the bed, and the bed was between them and the door. Very slowly Tom pressed open the door, trembling every time it creaked. When he judged that he might creep through on hands and knees, he put his head through and began.

"Why is the candle burning so badly?" said Aunt Polly. Tom hurried up. "Why, that door's open, I believe. Sid, go and shut it."

Tom disappeared under the bed just in time.

"But as I was saying," said Aunt Polly, "he wasn't

bad, only mischievous. He never meant to do any harm, and he was the best-hearted boy that ever lived." She began to cry.

"My Joe was the same. He was full of monkey-tricks, but always unselfish and kind. I whipped him for taking that cream, forgetting that I threw it out myself because it was sour. It is heartbreaking to think that I'll never see him again in this world, never, never, never, poor, ill-treated boy!" Mrs. Harper wept bitterly.

"I hope Tom is happier where he is," said Sid; "but if he'd been better in some ways——"

"*Sid!*" Tom knew that the old lady's eyes flashed, although he could not see them. "Don't say a word against my Tom, now that he's dead! Oh, Mrs. Harper, I don't know how to give him up! I don't know how to give him up!"

"God gives, and God takes away. But it's *so* hard. Oh, it's *so* hard! Only last Saturday my Joe made me jump with one of his noisy tricks, and I struck him. If he could do it again, I'd take him in my arms and bless him for it."

"Yes, yes, I know just how you feel, Mrs. Harper. Only yesterday my Tom filled the cat full of Pain-killer, and I did think that the creature would tear the house down. And, God forgive me, I slapped him, poor boy, poor, dead boy. But he's out of all his troubles now. And the last words I ever heard him say were to blame me——"

But this memory was too much for the old lady, and she broke down entirely. Tom was crying now, and more in pity of himself than of anybody else. He could hear Mary crying, and putting in a kindly word for him from time to time. Still, he was sufficiently moved by his aunt's grief to long to rush out and overcome her with the joy of his return, but he resisted the temptation. He went on listening and gathered that it was thought at first that the boys had been drowned while

having a swim. Then the small raft had been missed.
Next, it was remembered that the missing boys had
promised that the village would " hear something startling " soon. The opinion of most people was that the
boys had gone off on the raft and would appear at the
next town downstream; but at noon the raft had been
found against the bank five or six miles below the village. They must be drowned, otherwise hunger would
have driven them home. This was Wednesday night.
If the boys continued to be missing and if their bodies
were not recovered from the river before Sunday, all
hope would be given up and the funeral service would
be held on Sunday morning. Tom shivered.

Mrs. Harper wiped her eyes, said good night and left.
Aunt Polly was far more tender than usual in her good
night to Sid and Mary, who went off crying.

Aunt Polly knelt down and prayed for Tom so
earnestly and with such infinite love in her words and
her old, trembling voice that Tom's eyes were streaming with tears long before she had finished.

He had to keep still long after she had gone to bed,
for she was restless and kept on murmuring broken-
heartedly. But at last she lay still, only moaning a little
in her sleep. Now the boy stole out and stood regarding
her. His heart was full of pity for her. He took out
the bark roll and placed it by the candle. But something occurred to him, and he stood considering. A
smile lit up his face and he put the bark back in his
pocket. Then he bent over and kissed the faded lips,
and tiptoed out.

He went to the ferry-landing and walked boldly on
board the boat, for he knew that the watchman always
slept like a log. He untied the rowing-boat, slipped
into it and was soon rowing cautiously across the river.
He was tempted to capture it, but he knew that a
thorough search would be made for it and then they
might be discovered. So he tied it up as soon as he
landed and set off through the woods.

It was broad daylight before he found himself opposite the island sand-bar. He rested until the sun was well up and turning the surface of the great river into gold, and then entered the water. A little later he paused, dripping, on the edge of the camp.

" No, Tom's straight," he heard Joe say, " and he'll come back. He won't desert. He knows that would be shameful for a pirate, and Tom's too proud for that sort of thing. But I wonder what he's doing?"

" Well, the things are ours, aren't they?"

"Nearly, but not quite, Huck. The writing says that they are if he's not back for breakfast."

" Which he is!" exclaimed Tom, stepping grandly into camp.

A splendid breakfast was soon provided, and Tom described his adventures. They were a vain and boastful company of heroes when the tale was finished. Then Tom hid himself away to sleep till noon, and the other pirates got ready to fish and explore.

CHAPTER 18

HOMESICK: JOE "LOSES HIS KNIFE"

AFTER dinner, all the gang[1] set out to hunt for turtle[2] eggs on the sand-bar. They pushed sticks into the sand, and when they found a soft place they went down on their knees and dug with their hands. Sometimes they took fifty or sixty eggs out of one hole. They had a grand fried-egg feast that night, and another on Friday morning. After breakfast they dashed out on to the bar and chased each other round and round, and then

---

[1] A gang=a band of criminals.
[2] A turtle=a creature with a hard shell from which only the head, legs and tail appear.

continued their game out against the stiff current, which
swept their legs from under them from time to time and
greatly increased the fun. Now and then they stood in
a group and threw water in each other's faces with their
palms, gradually approaching each other with faces
turned aside and finally seizing each other and struggling until they all went under in confusion, and came
up blowing, laughing and gasping for breath at one and
the same time.

When they were exhausted, they would stretch out
on the hot, dry sand and cover themselves up with it,
and after a time dash for the water again and do the
same once more. Then they drew a ring in the sand
and had a circus, with three lion-tamers in it, as each
refused to have any other job.

Next they got their marbles and played various
games until they grew tired of this amusement. They
had another swim and a long rest. After this they
gradually wandered apart and began to gaze longingly
across the wide river at the village asleep in the sun.
Tom found himself writing *Becky* in the sand with his
big toe. He scratched it out and was angry with himself for his weakness.

But Joe was so homesick that he could hardly bear
the misery of it. Huck had a long face, too. Tom was
downhearted, but he tried hard not to show it. He had
a secret which he was not ready to tell yet, but if this
depression was not broken up soon he would have to
reveal it.

Tom suggested that they should go hunting for
pirates' treasure, chests of gold and silver, but the
others were not keen on doing so. Tom made other
suggestions, but they failed, too. It was discouraging
work. Joe sat digging a stick into the sand and looking
very gloomy.

"Oh, boys, let's give it up," said Joe finally. "I
want to go home. It's so lonely."

"Oh, no, Joe, you'll feel better soon. Just think of

the fishing here, and there isn't another swimming-place anywhere better than this."

"Swimming's no good. I don't seem to care for it, somehow, when there isn't anybody to say that I mustn't swim. I want to go home."

"Well, we'll let the cry-baby go home to its mother, won't we, Huck? Poor thing, does it want to see its mother? And so it shall. *You* like it here, don't you, Huck? We'll stay, won't we?"

Huck said "Y-e-s" without any heart in it.

"I'll never speak to you again as long as I live," said Joe, rising to collect his belongings. Soon, without a parting word, he began to walk slowly through the shallow water towards the Illinois bank. Tom's heart began to sink. He glanced at Huck. Huck dropped his eyes.

"I want to go, too, Tom," said he. "It was getting lonely and now it'll be worse. Let's go too, Tom."

"Well, go. Who's hindering you?"

Huck walked sorrowfully away and Tom watched them moving slowly on. Tom suddenly noticed that everything had become very lonely and still. He made one final struggle with his pride, and then dashed after his friends.

"Wait! Wait!" he shouted. "I want to tell you something!"

They stopped and turned round. When he reached them, he began unfolding his secret and they listened gloomily till at last they understood his plan. Then they gave a cheer and said that it was marvellous. They assured him that they would not have left him if he had told them before. Tom made up an excuse, but his real reason had been the fear that not even the secret would keep them with him any very great length of time, and so he had meant to hold it in reserve as a last persuasion.

The boys came gaily back and continued their sports, talking all the time about Tom's plan and admiring the cleverness of it. After a delicious egg-and-fish dinner, Tom said that he wanted to learn how to smoke. Joe said that he would like to try, too. So Huck filled pipes, and they stretched themselves out on their elbows and began to puff cautiously and with little confidence. The smoke had an unpleasant taste and they gasped a little.

" Why, it's easy ! " Tom said. " If I'd known that *this* was all, I'd have learnt long ago."

" So would I," said Joe. " It's just nothing. I believe I could smoke this pipe all day. *I* don't feel sick."

" Neither do I," said Tom. " *I* could smoke all day, but I bet you Jeff Thatcher couldn't."

" Jeff Thatcher ! Why, he'd fall down with just two puffs ! "

" I say, boys, don't say anything about it, and some time when the boys are around I'll come up to you and say, ' Joe, have you got a pipe? I want a smoke ! ' And you'll say, in a careless way, as if it was nothing, you'll say, ' Yes, I've got my *old* pipe, and another one, but my tobacco isn't very good.' And I'll say, ' Oh, that's all right, if it's *strong* enough.' And then you'll take out the pipes and we'll light them as if it was nothing. How they will stare ! "

" That will be grand, Tom ! I wish it was now ! "

So the talk ran on, but presently it began to drag a little. The silences widened. Spitting marvellously increased. Fountains seemed to be at work inside their cheeks. Both the boys were looking very pale and miserable now. Joe's pipe dropped from his fingers. Tom's followed.

" I've lost my knife," said Joe faintly. " I think I'd better go and find it."

Tom rose unsteadily and said with trembling lips, " I'll help you. You go over that way and I'll search by the spring. No, you needn't come, Huck. We can find it."

So Huck sat down again and waited an hour. Then he found it lonely and went to find his companions. They were wide apart in the woods, both very pale, both fast asleep. But something informed him that if they had had any trouble they had got rid of it.

They were not very talkative at supper that night. They had a humble look. When Huck prepared his pipe after the meal and was going to prepare theirs, they told him not to. They were not feeling very well. Something they ate at dinner had upset them.

CHAPTER 14

THE STORM

ABOUT midnight Joe awoke and called the boys. There was a weighty stillness in the air that seemed to threaten something. The boys sought the friendly companionship of the fire, in spite of the dead heat of the breathless air. They sat still and expectant. Beyond the light of the fire everything was swallowed up in the blackness. Presently a weak flash of lightning dimly lit the trees for a moment and vanished. Another came, a little stronger. Then another. Then a faint moan came sighing through the branches and the boys trembled, fancying that some spirit of the night had gone by. There was a pause. Now a terrible flash turned night into day and showed, separate and distinct, every little grass-blade that grew about their feet. It showed three white, startled faces, too. A deep roll of thunder went crashing across the sky and lost itself in the distance. A cold breeze sprang up. It shook all the leaves and scattered ashes about the fire. Another fierce flash lit up the forest, and a crash followed that seemed to tear the tree-tops right over the boys' heads. They held on to each other in terror in the thick gloom that followed.

A few big raindrops fell upon the leaves.

"Quick, boys, go for the tent!" exclaimed Tom.

They leapt away, stumbling over roots in the dark, each dashing in a different direction. A furious wind roared through the trees, making everything sing as it went. One blinding flash after another came, and roll upon roll of deafening thunder. And now the rain poured down and the rising wind drove it in sheets along the ground. The boys cried out to each other, but the howling wind and the roaring thunder drowned their voices utterly. However, one by one they staggered in at last, and took shelter under the tent, cold, frightened and streaming with water. The old sail beat about so furiously that they could not talk, even if the other noises had allowed them. The storm rose higher and higher, and presently the sail tore loose from its fastenings and went flying away on the wind. The boys seized each other's hands and fled, with many stumblings and bruises, to the shelter of a great oak that stood upon the river bank.

Now the battle was at its highest. Under the ceaseless flashes that flamed in the sky, everything below—the bending trees, the river white with foam, the dim outlines of the cliffs on the other side seen through the racing clouds and the veil of rain—stood out in clean-cut and shadowless distinctness. From time to time some giant trees yielded in the fight and fell crashing through the younger growth. The thunder came now in ear-splitting, explosive bursts, pitilessly keen, and unspeakably awful. The storm ended with one gigantic effort that seemed likely to tear the island to pieces, burn it up, drown it to the tree-tops, blow it away and deafen every creature in it, all at one and the same moment. It was a wild night for homeless young heads to be out in.

But at last the battle was over, and the forces of Nature retired, with weaker and weaker threats, and peace returned. The boys went back to camp a good deal awed; but they found that there was still something to be thankful for, because the great tree, which had been the shelter of their beds, was a ruin now, split by the lightning.

Everything in the camp was wet through, the camp-fire as well. Here was a disaster, for they were wet to the skin and shivering. However, they discovered that the fire had eaten so far up the great log against which it had been built that a few inches had escaped wetting. They patiently worked at it with leaves and bark gathered from the under-sides of sheltered logs until they persuaded it to burn again. Then they piled on great dead branches till they had a roaring blaze. They dried their food and had a feast. After that they sat by the fire and glorified their midnight adventure until morning, for there was not a dry spot to sleep on anywhere around.

As the sun grew stronger, the boys felt sleepy and they went out on the sand-bar and lay down. They were soon burnt out by the sun, and wearily began to prepare breakfast. After the meal they felt stiff-jointed and a little homesick once more. Tom saw the signs and tried to cheer up the pirates as well as he could. But they cared nothing for marbles, or circuses, or swimming, or anything. He proposed that they should stop being pirates for a time and be Red Indians for a change. They were attracted by this idea. It was not long before they were stripped and striped from head to heel with black mud, all of them chiefs, of course, and then they went dashing through the woods to attack an English settlement.

Afterwards they separated into three rival tribes and sprang out upon each other from hiding-places with dreadful war-cries, and killed and skinned each other by thousands. It was a bloody day, and therefore was a satisfactory one.

They assembled in camp towards supper-time, hungry and happy. But now a difficulty arose. Indian tribes at war with each other could not break bread together without first making peace, and this was simply an impossibility without smoking a pipe of peace. Two of the Redskins almost wished that they had remained pirates. However, there was no other way, so with as much cheerfulness as they could pretend they called for the pipe and took their puff, as it passed, with proper ceremony.

They were glad that they had become Redskins, for they found that they could now smoke a little without having to go and hunt for a lost knife. They did not get sick enough to be seriously uncomfortable. They practised cautiously after supper with fair success, and so they spent a joyful evening.

CHAPTER 15

BACK FROM THE DEAD

But there was no joyfulness in the village that Saturday afternoon. The Harpers and Aunt Polly's family were overcome with grief. An unusual quiet possessed the village. The villagers talked little; but they sighed often. The Saturday holiday seemed a burden to the children. They were not interested in their sports and gradually gave them up.

In the afternoon Becky Thatcher found herself wandering about the deserted school-yard, and feeling very unhappy; but she saw nothing there to comfort her.

Presently she stopped and said to herself:

" It was just here. Oh, if he was to do it again, I wouldn't say that he was very smart; I wouldn't say that for the world. But he's gone now, and I'll never, never, never see him any more."

This thought made her burst into tears, and she

walked slowly away. Then a group of boys and girls, Tom's and Joe's playmates, came by and stood looking over the fence and talking in respectful tones of how Tom did so and so the last time they saw him, and how Joe said this and that.

When the Sunday-school hour was finished the next morning, the church bell began to ring very slowly and solemnly, instead of ringing in the usual way. The villagers began to gather, staying a moment in the entrance of the church to converse in whispers about the sad event. None could remember when the little church had been so full before. There was finally a waiting pause, and then Aunt Polly entered with Sid and Mary, followed by the Harper family, all in deep black. The villagers and the old minister as well rose respectfully and stood until the mourners were seated in front. The minister prayed, and a moving, sacred song was sung.

As the service proceeded, the minister drew such pictures of the charming ways and the rare promise of the lost children that every soul there, thinking that he recognized these pictures, felt sad in remembering that he had only seen faults in the poor boys. The minister described some good deeds in the lives of the departed which showed their sweet, generous natures. The villagers became more and more moved as the sad tale went on, till at last there was not a dry eye in the whole church.

Among the unused seats upstairs there was a slight noise which nobody noticed. A moment later the church door creaked. The minister raised his streaming eyes above his handkerchief and stood as if turned to stone, gazing in the direction of the door. All turned round, rose to their feet and stared as if they could not believe their eyes while the three dead boys came marching up the middle of the church, Tom leading, Joe next, and Huck last. They had been hidden upstairs, listening to their own funeral service !

Aunt Polly, Mary and the Harpers threw themselves upon their recovered ones, covered them with kisses, and poured out thanksgivings, while poor Huck stood ashamed and uncomfortable in his rags, not knowing what to do or where to hide from so many unfriendly eyes. He started to creep away, but Tom seized him and said:

" Aunt Polly, it isn't fair. Somebody must be glad to see Huck."

" And so they shall! I'm glad to see him, poor, motherless boy!" And the loving attentions which Aunt Polly showered upon him made him more uncomfortable than he was before.

Suddenly the minister shouted at the top of his voice:

" ' Praise God from whom all blessings flow.' *Sing!* And put your hearts into it! "

And they did. While the grand old song shook the roof, Tom Sawyer the Pirate looked around upon the envying children about him, and confessed in his heart that this was the proudest moment of his life.

CHAPTER 16

TOM'S " DREAM ": BECKY'S REVENGE

THAT was the great secret—the plan to return home with his brother pirates and attend their own funerals. They had sailed over to the Missouri side on a log at twilight on Saturday, landing five or six miles below the village. They had slept in the woods till nearly daylight, and had then crept through the back lanes and finished their sleep upstairs in the church.

At breakfast on Monday morning Aunt Polly and Mary were very loving to Tóm and very attentive to his wants. There was an unusual amount of talk, in the course of which Aunt Polly said:

"Well, perhaps it was a fine joke, Tom, but it was cruel to let me suffer so. If you could come over on a log to attend your funeral, you could have come over and told me that you weren't dead."

"Yes, you could have done that," said Mary; "and I believe you would if you had thought of it."

"Would you, Tom?" asked Aunt Polly, rather sadly.

"I—well, I don't know. It would have spoiled everything."

"Tom, I hoped you loved me as much as that," said Aunt Polly in a grieved tone that discomforted the boy. "It would have been something if you'd cared enough to think of it, even if you didn't do it. Tom, you'll look back some day, when it's too late, and wish you'd cared a little more for me when it would have cost you so little."

"Now, auntie, you know that I do care for you."

"I'd know it better if you showed me that you cared."

"I wish now I'd thought," said Tom regretfully; "but I dreamed about you, anyway. That's something, isn't it?"

"It isn't much; a cat does that. But it's better than nothing. What did you dream?"

"Why, Wednesday night I dreamt that you were sitting over there by the bed, and Sid was sitting by the wood-box, and Mary next to him."

"Well, so we did. So we always do."

"And I dreamt that Joe Harper's mother was here."

"Why, she was here! Did you dream any more?"

"Oh, lots. But it's so dim now."

"Well, try to remember. Can't you?"

"Somehow it seemed to me that the wind—the wind blew the—the——"

"Try harder, Tom! The wind did blow something. Yes?"

Tom pressed his fingers on his forehead for an anxious minute and then said:

"I've got it now! I've got it now! It blew the candle! And it seemed to me that you said, 'Why, I believe that that door——'"

"Good heavens! Go on, Tom, go on!"

"Just let me think a moment; just a moment. Oh, yes! You said that you believed the door was open."

"That's as true as I'm sitting here! I did, didn't I, Mary? Go on!"

"And then—and then—well, I won't be certain, but it seemed as if you made Sid go and—and——"

"Well? Well? What did I make him do, Tom?"

"You made him—you—oh, you made him shut it!"

"Goodness gracious! I've never heard anything like that in all my days! There is some truth in dreams. Serena Harper shall know of this before I'm an hour older. When I tell her about my dreams she says, 'Rubbish!' and 'Fancies!' Go on, Tom."

"Oh, it's all getting as bright as day now. Next you said that I wasn't bad, only mischievous——"

"And so I did! Well, well! Go on, Tom!"

"And then you began to cry."

"I did. I did. Not for the first time, either. And then?"

"Then Mrs. Harper began to cry, and said Joe was just the same, and she wished that she hadn't whipped him for taking the cream which she'd thrown away herself——"

"Good Lord! Tom, this is a miracle! Goodness gracious! Go on, Tom!"

"Then Sid said—he said——"

"I don't think I said anything," said Sid.

"Yes, you did, Sid," said Mary.

"Shut your mouths and let Tom go on! What did he say, Tom?"

"He said—I think he said he hoped I was happier where I had gone to, but if I'd been better sometimes——"

"There, do you hear that? His very words!"

"And you made him shut up."

"I did! An angel must have shown you all that, Tom. There was an angel with you!"

"And Mrs. Harper told about Joe making her jump, and you told about Peter and the Pain-killer——"

"As true as I'm sitting here."

"Then there was a lot of talk about having the funeral on Sunday, and then you and Mrs. Harper cried, and she went."

"It happened just so! Tom, you couldn't have told it better if you'd seen it! And then what?"

"And then I thought you prayed for me, and I could see you and hear every word. You went to bed, and I was so sorry that I wrote on a piece of bark, ' We're not dead; we're only being pirates,' and I put it by the candle; and then you looked so good, lying there asleep, that I thought I went and leaned over and kissed you."

"Did you, Tom, did you? I forgive you everything for that!" And when she threw her arms about him he felt the guiltiest of villains.

"Here's a big apple I've been saving for you, Tom, if you were ever found again. Now off you go, all of you. You've wasted enough of my time."

The children left for school and the old lady went to call on Mrs. Harper and conquer her disbelief with Tom's marvellous dream.

What a hero Tom was now! He did not go jumping and dancing, but stepped with his chest out like a pirate who felt that the public eye was on him. He tried not to seem to see the looks or hear the remarks as he passed along, but they were food and drink[1] to him. Smaller boys than himself flocked at his heels, as proud to be seen with him as if he had been the drummer at the head of a procession, or an elephant leading a circus

---

[1] Food and drink to him = essential to him; something that he liked to have.

into town. Boys of his own size pretended not to know that he had been away at all, but in reality they were eaten up with envy. They would have given anything to have that dark, sunburnt skin of his, and his glittering fame.

At school the children were so full of admiration for Tom and Joe that the two heroes soon became unbearably vain. Finally, when they got out their pipes and went puffing around, the very height of glory was reached.

Tom decided that he could be independent of Becky Thatcher now. Glory was sufficient. He would live for glory. Now that he was distinguished, perhaps she would be wanting to be friends again. Well, she would see that he could be as proud as some other people. Presently she arrived. Tom pretended not to see her. He moved away, joined a group of boys and girls and began to talk. Soon he observed that she was running gaily to and fro pretending to chase schoolmates, and screaming with laughter when she made a capture, but he noticed that she always made her captures in his neighbourhood. After a time she gave up playing and moved hesitatingly about, glancing occasionally at Tom. Then she observed that Tom was talking more particularly to Amy Lawrence than to anyone else. She grew disturbed and uneasy at once. She tried to go away, but her feet led her to the group instead.

" Mary, I want to tell you about the picnic,"[1] said Becky to a girl almost at Tom's elbow.

" Oh, who's going to give it? "

" My mother's going to let me have one."

" I hope she will let me come."

" She will. The picnic's for me. She'll let anybody come that I want, and I want you."

" That's nice of you. When is it going to be? "

" Soon. Perhaps in the holidays."

" Oh, won't it be fun ! Are you going to invite all

---

[1] A picnic = a short trip into the country with a meal out of doors.

the boys and girls?"

"Yes, everyone who is a friend of mine, or wants to be," and she glanced at Tom, but he talked on to Amy Lawrence about the storm on the island, and how the lightning tore the great tree to bits, while he was "standing within three feet of it."

With a clapping of joyful hands all the group begged for invitations, except Tom and Amy. Then Tom walked off with Amy. Becky's eyes filled with tears. She went as soon as she could, and sat alone till the bell rang. Then she dried her eyes, held up her head and said that she knew what she would do.

During the interval Tom continued in the company of Amy and kept wandering about to find Becky in order to make her feel angry. At last he caught sight of her. She was sitting on a little bench behind the school, looking at a picture-book with Alfred Temple. So deeply interested were they, and so close together were their heads over the book, that they did not seem to notice anything else. Jealousy ran red-hot through Tom. He called himself a fool for throwing away the chance of becoming friends again which Becky had offered. Amy's happy talk became unbearable. Tom spoke vaguely about some things which he had to do and hastened away.

"She thinks that that over-dressed fool is better than I am," he thought, grinding his teeth. "Oh, all right. I gave him a beating the first time I saw him, and I'll do it again."

He went through the motions of fighting an imaginary boy, hitting the air and kicking and pulling.

"Oh, you've had enough, have you? You have, have you? Now, let that be a lesson to you!"

And so the imaginary beating was finished to his satisfaction.

Tom fled home at noon. His conscience could not bear any more of Amy's grateful happiness, and his jealousy made the sight of Becky and Alfred Temple together unbearable, too. Becky looked at some more pictures with Alfred, but no Tom came to suffer. She grew miserable, and when Alfred kept on exclaiming, "Oh, here's a nice one! Look at this!" she lost patience and said, "Oh, I don't care for them," and got up and walked away.

Alfred went thoughtfully into the deserted school. He easily guessed the truth. The girl had simply made use of him to annoy Tom Sawyer. He wished that there was some way of getting that boy into trouble without much risk to himself. His eye fell on Tom's spelling-book. Here was his opportunity. He opened it at the lesson for the afternoon and poured ink upon the page. Becky, glancing in at a window behind him, saw him and moved away quickly. She hurried away, intending to find Tom and tell him. Tom would be thankful and their troubles would be ended. Before she was half-way home, however, she changed her mind. She thought of Tom's treatment of her when she was talking about the picnic, and she determined to let him be punished on account of the damaged spelling-book and to hate him for ever, too.

CHAPTER 17

AUNT POLLY'S TEARS

WHEN Tom arrived home his aunt said:

"Tom, I'd like to skin you alive!"

"Auntie, what have I done?"

"Well, you've done enough. I went over to Serena Harper like an old fool, expecting to make her believe all that rubbish about that dream, and she'd found out from Joe that you'd been over here and heard all that talk. It makes me feel so bad to think that you could let me go to Serena Harper and make such a fool of myself, and never say a word."

This was a different view of the matter. His smartness of the morning had seemed to Tom a good joke. It merely looked shameful now. He hung his head. Then he said:

"Auntie, I wish I hadn't done it, but I didn't think."

"Oh, child, you never think. You never think of anything but your own selfishness. You could think of coming all the way from Jackson's Island in the night to laugh at our troubles and of deceiving me with a lie about a dream, but you couldn't think of pitying us and saving us from sorrow."

"Auntie, I know now that it was wrong, but I didn't mean to do wrong. I didn't, really. And besides, I didn't come over here to laugh at you that night."

"What did you come for, then?"

"To tell you not to be anxious about us, because we hadn't been drowned."

"Tom, Tom, I would be the most thankful person in the world if I could believe that you ever had such a good intention; but you know that you never came for that purpose, and I know it, Tom."

"Really I did, auntie; I swear that I did."

"Oh, Tom, don't lie. It only makes things a hundred times worse."

"It isn't a lie, auntie. It's the truth. I wanted to save you from feeling unhappy. That was all that made me come."

"I'd give the whole world to believe that. I could forgive everything if that was true, Tom. But it isn't reasonable, because why didn't you tell me, child?"

"Why, you see, auntie, when you began talking about the funeral, I thought of coming and hiding in the church. It seemed such a wonderful idea that I couldn't give it up. So I just put the bark back in my pocket and kept quiet."

"The bark?"

"The bark which I wrote on to tell you that we'd

gone pirating. I wish, now, that you'd woke up when I kissed you; I do, really."

The hard lines in his aunt's face softened and she gazed at the boy tenderly.

" *Did* you kiss me, Tom? "

" Why, yes, I did."

" Are you sure you did, Tom? "

" Quite sure, auntie."

" Why did you kiss me, Tom? "

" Because I loved you so, and you lay there moaning, and I was so sorry."

The words sounded like truth. A lump rose in the old lady's throat and she said unsteadily:

" Kiss me again, Tom! Now run off to school and don't trouble me any more."

The moment he had gone, she ran to the cupboard and took out the ruined coat in which Tom had gone pirating. Then she stopped with it in her hand and said to herself:

" No, I daren't. Poor boy, I think he's lied about it; but it's a good lie, it's made me feel happier. I hope God will forgive him, because such a lie shows that he has a good heart. But I don't want to find out that it's a lie. I won't look."

She put the coat away, and stood thoughtfully a minute. Twice she put out her hand to take the coat again, and twice she drew back. Once more she stretched out her hand, and this time she strengthened herself with the thought: " It's a good lie; I won't let it grieve me." So she felt in the coat pocket. A moment later she was reading Tom's piece of bark through flowing tears and saying:

" I could forgive the boy, now, if he'd committed a million sins! "

CHAPTER 18

"HOW COULD YOU BE SO NOBLE!"

THERE was something about Aunt Polly's manner when she kissed Tom that swept away his feeling of depression. He set off for school and had the luck to meet Becky Thatcher. When he was happy, he could never be angry with anyone and so he said:

"Becky, I behaved very badly to-day, and I'm sorry. Let us be friends."

The girl stopped and looked him scornfully in the face.

"Please don't speak to me, Mr. Thomas Sawyer."

She held up her head proudly and passed on. Tom was stunned. He presently saw her in the school-yard, and made a stinging remark. She fired one in return and could hardly wait for school to begin, so impatient was she to see Tom punished for the damaged spelling-book.

Poor girl, she did not know that she would soon be in trouble herself. The teacher, Mr. Dobbins, had reached middle age with an unsatisfied ambition. The goal of his desires was to be a doctor, but fate had arranged that he should be nothing higher than a village schoolmaster. Every day he took a mysterious book out of his desk and studied it at times. Every pupil in the school was longing to have a look at it, but the chance never came. Now as Becky was passing by the desk, which stood near the door, she noticed that the key was in the lock. It was a precious moment. She glanced round, found herself alone and the next instant she had the book in her hands. She noted that it was Professor Somebody's *Health and Disease* and began to turn the pages. At that moment a shadow fell on the page and Tom Sawyer stepped in at the door. Becky snatched at the book to close it and had the misfortune to tear a page. She thrust the book into the desk, turned the key and burst out crying with shame and annoyance.

"Tom Sawyer, how could you be so horrid! Creeping up to see what one's looking at."

"How could *I* know that you were looking at anything?"

"You ought to be ashamed of yourself. I know that you're going to tell the teacher about me; and oh, what shall I do? I'll be punished, and I have never been punished in school!" And she rushed out of the classroom in a storm of tears.

In a few moments the teacher arrived and lessons began. Soon the spelling-book discovery was made. Becky thought for a moment of telling about Alfred Temple, but she forced herself to keep quiet, because, she said to herself, "He'll tell about me tearing the book. I wouldn't say a word, not even to save his life!"

Tom took his punishment and went back to his seat not at all broken-hearted, for he thought that he might have upset the ink on the spelling-book himself.

A whole hour passed by. Then Mr. Dobbins unlocked his desk and reached for his book, but seemed undecided whether to take it out or leave it. Most of the pupils glanced up idly, but there were two who watched his movements closely. Mr. Dobbins fingered his book thoughtfully for a time, then took it out and settled himself in his chair to read.

Tom glanced at Becky. The anxious expression on her face made him forget his quarrel with her. Quick! Something must be done! He would run and snatch the book, spring through the door and fly! But he hesitated; his chance was lost; the teacher had opened the book. The next moment he faced the school. His stern gaze made even the innocent tremble. There was a silence while one might count ten. Then he spoke:

" Who tore this book? "

There was not a sound. One could have heard a pin drop. The teacher searched face after face for signs of guilt.

" Benjamin Rogers, did you tear this book? "

A denial. Another pause.

" Joseph Harper, did you? "

Another denial. Tom's uneasiness grew as the teacher examined the rows of boys, considered for a moment and then turned to the girls.

" Amy Lawrence? "

A shake of the head.

" Gracie Miller? "

The same sign.

" Susan Harper, did you do this? "

Another negative. The next girl was Becky Thatcher. Tom was trembling from head to foot with excitement and a sense of the hopelessness of the situation.

" Rebecca Thatcher " (Tom glanced at her face; it was white with terror) " did you tear—no, look me in the face—did you tear this book? "

A thought shot like lightning through Tom's brain. He sprang to his feet and shouted:

" *I* did it ! "

The pupils stared, astounded at Tom's foolishness. When he stepped forward to his punishment, the surprise, the gratitude, the worship that shone upon him out of Becky's eyes seemed reward enough for a hundred whippings. He took without a murmur the most severe punishment that even Mr. Dobbins had ever given.

Tom went to bed that night planning revenge against Alfred Temple, for Becky had told him all; but even the longing for revenge had to give way soon to pleasanter thoughts, and he fell asleep at last with Becky's words still in his ear:

" Tom, how *could* you be so noble ! "

CHAPTER 19

PRIZE DAY

THE summer holiday was approaching. The teacher, always severe, grew severer than ever, for he wanted the school to do well on Prize Day. His stick was seldom idle now, and Mr. Dobbins's punishments were very energetic ones, too. Although he carried, under his false hair, a perfectly hairless and shiny head, he had only reached middle age and showed no signs of weakness. As the great day approached, he seemed to take a fierce pleasure in punishing the least misbehaviour. The result was that the smallest boys spent their days in terror and their nights in planning revenge. At last they hit upon a plan which promised a glorious victory. As the teacher lodged at the sign-painter's house, the boys asked the sign-painter's son to help them. He agreed at once, because he, too, disliked the teacher. Mrs. Dobbins would go on a visit to the country in a few days, and there would be nothing to interfere with the plan. Mr. Dobbins always prepared himself for great occasions, such as Prize Day, by having a little too much to drink, and the sign-painter's boy said that he was confident that he could carry out his part of the plan while the teacher was having a short sleep in his chair. Then he would have him awakened at the right time and hurried away to school.

The great occasion arrived. At eight in the evening the school was brightly lighted and decorated with flowers. The teacher sat in his armchair upon a platform, with his blackboard behind him. He was very cheerful. In front of him were rows of chairs occupied by the most important people of the town and by the parents of the pupils. To his left was another platform, upon which were seated the scholars who were to take part in the exercises of the evening. The rest of the schoolroom was filled with the other pupils.

The exercises began. A very little boy stood up and sheepishly recited " You'd scarcely expect one of my age, to speak in public on the stage," etc., accompanying himself with the painfully exact and stiff motions which a machine might have made, supposing that machine to be a trifle out of order.

A little shamefaced girl murmured " Mary had a little lamb," etc., was loudly applauded, and sat down blushing and happy.

Tom Sawyer stepped forward with vain confidence and rushed into the " Give me liberty or give me death " speech with fine fury, and broke down in the middle of it. The teacher frowned, and this completed the disaster. Tom struggled for a time, and then retired, utterly defeated. There was a weak attempt at applause, but it died early.

" The boy stood on the burning deck " and other masterpieces of recitation followed. Then there were reading exercises and a spelling fight. The small Latin class recited with credit.

The highlight of the evening, original compositions by the young ladies, now came. Each in her turn stepped forward to the edge of the platform, cleared her throat, held up her paper, which was tied with pretty ribbon, and proceeded to read with special attention to expression and punctuation.

The first prize was won by a black-eyed, black-haired young lady with a mournful expression. Her composition on " A Vision " was considered the finest effort of the evening, and the mayor of the village, after delivering the prize to her, made a warm speech, in which he said that it was the finest thing he had ever listened to and that it was worthy of the country's greatest statesmen.

Now the teacher put his chair aside, turned his back to the audience, and began to draw a map of America on the blackboard, upon which to exercise the geography class. But he did it very badly, because his hand was unsteady. A low laugh ran round the room. He knew what was wrong and set himself to right it. He rubbed out lines and remade them. But the laughter grew louder, and with good reason. There was a store-room above and the entrance to it was just above his head. Down through this opening came a cat hanging from a string tied round her body. She had a rag fastened about her head and jaws to prevent her from making a noise. As she slowly descended, she curved upwards and seized the string with her claws,[1] then swung downwards and clawed at the air. The laughter grew louder and louder. The cat was within six inches of the teacher's head. Down, down, a little lower, and she seized his false hair with her desperate claws, held it, and was snatched up into the store-room in an instant, with her prize still in her possession! And how the light blazed from the teacher's hairless head, for the sign-painter's boy had *covered it with gold paint!*

That broke up the meeting. The boys had had their revenge.

CHAPTER 20

THE TRIAL OF POTTER

Tom soon began to wonder why his longed-for holiday was not as exciting as he had hoped.

A circus came. After it had gone, the boys had a circus of their own in tents made of old rugs. The price of admission was three pins for boys and two for girls. After three days, their circus was given up.

There were some boys' and girls' parties, but they were so few and delightful that they only made the emptiness between harder to bear.

---

[1] Claws = the pointed nails of an animal or bird.

Becky Thatcher was away with her parents, and so there was no bright side to life anywhere.

Tom fell ill. When he had recovered, he wandered down the street and found Jim Hollis acting as judge in a court composed of children. He was trying a cat for murder, in the presence of her victim, a bird.

Murder was the chief subject of conversation in the village, for the murder trial came on in court. Tom took Huck aside to have a talk with him. It would be a relief to unseal his tongue. Moreover, he wanted to assure himself that Huck had not betrayed the secret.

" Huck, have you told anybody about that? "

" About what? "

" You know. "

" Oh, of course I haven't. "

" Huck, they couldn't force you to tell, could they? "

" Force me to tell? Why, if I wanted that half-breed devil to kill me they could force me to tell. "

As twilight drew on, they found themselves hanging about the neighbourhood of the little prison, and they did as they had often done before; they gave Potter some tobacco and matches through the bars. They felt very cowardly and treacherous when Potter said:

" You've been very good to me, boys. I often say to myself, ' I used to mend all the boys' kites and things and show them the best fishing-places, and befriend them when I could, and now they've forgotten me when I'm in trouble. But Tom hasn't, and Huck hasn't.' Shake hands. Yours will come through the bars, but mine's too big. Little hands, and weak, but they've helped me a lot, and they'd help me more if they could. "

Tom went home miserable, and his dreams that night were full of horrors. The next day and the day after he hung about the court. At the end of the second day the village talk was that Redskin Joe's evidence stood firm and unshaken and that there was not the slightest doubt what the jury's verdict would be.

Tom was out late that night and came to bed through the window. He was in a state of great excitement. It was hours before he got to sleep.

All the village flocked to the court the next morning, for this was to be the great day. After a long wait the jury took their places. Soon afterwards, Potter, pale and timid, was brought in and seated where all curious eyes could stare at him. No less noticeable was Redskin Joe's evil face. Then the Judge and the Sheriff arrived. The usual whisperings among the lawyers and the gathering together of papers followed. These details and the accompanying delays gave an impressive sense of expectation.

Now a witness was called who said that he found Potter washing in a stream at an early hour on the morning when the murder was discovered and that he immediately crept away. After some questioning, the lawyer for the prosecution[1] said:

" Examine the witness."

The lawyer for the defence said:

" I have no questions to ask him."

The next witness described the finding of the knife near the body. The lawyer for the prosecution said:

" Examine the witness."

" I have no questions to ask him," Potter's lawyer replied.

A third witness swore that he had often seen the knife in Potter's possession.

" Examine the witness."

Potter's lawyer refused to question him.

The faces of the audience began to show annoyance. Did this lawyer mean to throw away the prisoner's life without an effort to save him?

Every detail of what occurred in the graveyard that memorable morning was described by trustworthy witnesses, but none of them was cross-examined by

[1] To prosecute = to take action against in a court of law.

Potter's lawyer.

The lawyer for the prosecution now said:

" By the oaths of citizens whose word is above suspicion, we have shown beyond all possibility of doubt that this awful crime was committed by the prisoner."

A groan escaped from Potter, and there was a painful silence in court. The lawyer for the defence rose and addressed the Judge:

" Your Honour, in our remarks at the opening of the trial we showed that we intended to prove that the prisoner did this fearful deed while under the influence of drink. We have changed our mind. We shall not offer that excuse." Turning to the clerk, he said, " Call Tom Sawyer."

Everyone in court looked both amazed and puzzled. Tom, looking rather frightened, rose and took his place upon the stand. He swore the oath.

" Thomas Sawyer, where were you on the seventeenth of June, about the hour of midnight?"

Tom glanced at Redskin Joe's iron face and his tongue refused to move. The audience listened breathless, but the words would not come. After a few moments, however, the boy got a little of his strength back, and he managed to put enough of it into his voice to make part of the court hear.

" In the graveyard."

" A trifle louder, please. Don't be afraid. You were——"

" In the graveyard."

A scornful smile passed across Redskin Joe's face.

" Were you anywhere near Horse Williams's grave?"

" Yes, sir."

" Speak up a trifle louder. How near were you?"

" As near as I am to you."

" Were you hidden or not?"

" Hidden."

" Where?"

" Behind the trees on the edge of the grave."

Redskin Joe gave a slight start.

" Did you carry anything there with you? "

Tom hesitated and looked confused.

" Speak out, my boy. What did you take there? "

" Only a—a—dead cat."

There was some laughter, which the Judge checked.
" We shall produce the remains of that cat as evidence. Now, my boy, tell us everything that occurred. Tell it in your own way. Don't omit anything, and don't be afraid."

Tom began, hesitatingly at first, but soon his words flowed more and more easily. With parted lips the audience listened to his terrible tale.

" —and as the doctor brought the board down and Potter fell, Redskin Joe jumped with the knife and——"

Crash! As quick as lightning, the half-breed sprang towards a window, tore his way through all who tried to stop him, and was gone!

Tom was a hero once more, the pet of the old and the envy of the young. His name was even printed, for the village newspaper reported the part he had played.

Tom's days were days of glory, but his nights were seasons of horror. Redskin Joe was present in all his dreams and always with a fatal gleam in his eye. Nothing could persuade the boy to go out of doors after sunset. Poor Huck was in the same state of terror, for Tom had told the whole story to the lawyer the night before the trial, and Huck feared that his share in the matter might be found out. Since Tom's conscience had driven him to betray his oath, Huck's confidence in the human race had practically vanished. During the day Potter's gratitude made Tom feel glad that he had spoken, but at night he wished that he had said nothing.

Rewards were offered, the country was searched, but Redskin Joe was not found.

The days went slowly by, and each day Tom felt a little less afraid.

CHAPTER 21

DIGGING FOR TREASURE

THERE comes a time in the life of every normal boy when he is filled with a desire to go somewhere and dig for hidden treasure. This desire suddenly came upon Tom one day. He failed to find Joe Harper, and Ben Rogers had gone fishing, but he stumbled upon Huck Finn the Red-handed. Tom took him aside and revealed the matter to him privately.

" Where shall we dig? " asked Huck.

" Oh, almost anywhere."

" Why, is it hidden all around? "

" No, of course it's not. It's hidden in very special places, Huck. It's sometimes on islands, sometimes in rotten chests under the end of a limb of an old, dead tree, just where the shadow falls at midnight, but mostly under the floor in haunted houses."[1]

" Who hides it? "

" Why, robbers, of course! Who do you think? Teachers? "

" Don't they come back for it? "

" No, they think they will, but they generally forget the marks, or else they die. Anyway, it lies there a long time and gets rusty. Then somebody finds an old, yellow paper that tells one how to find the marks, a paper that has to be studied for about a week because it's mostly signs."

" Have you got one of those papers, Tom? "

" No."

" Well, then, how are you going to find out the

[1] A haunted house = a house in which the spirits of the dead appear to the living.

marks?"

"I don't want any marks. They always bury it under a haunted house, or on an island, or under a dead tree with one limb sticking out. There are lots of trees with dead limbs sticking out, hundreds of them."

"Is it under all of them?"

"How you talk! No!"

"Then how do you know which one to go for?"

"Go for all of them."

"Why, Tom, it will take all the summer!"

"Well, that doesn't matter. Suppose you find a pot with a hundred dollars in it, or a rotten chest full of diamonds. Would you like that?"

Huck's eyes glowed.

"That's fine, Tom, fine enough for me. Just give me the hundred dollars, and I won't want any diamonds."

"All right. But I won't turn my nose up at diamonds. Some of them are worth twenty dollars each. There aren't any worth less than a dollar. Haven't you ever seen one, Huck?"

"I don't think so."

"Oh, kings have bags of them."

"Well, I don't know any kings, Tom."

"I know you don't. But if you went to Europe, you'd see heaps of them."

"Are they in heaps?"

"In heaps? No!"

"Well, why did you say they were?"

"I only meant that you'd see a lot of them—not in heaps, of course. Why should they want to be in heaps?"

"All right. But where are you going to dig first?"

"Suppose we try that old dead-limb tree on the hill the other side of Still-House stream?"

"All right."

So they got a rusty pick and a spade and set out on their three-mile walk. They arrived hot and breathless and threw themselves down in the shade to rest. Then they worked and sweated for half an hour. There was no result. They laboured another half-hour. There was still no result.

" Do they always bury it as deep as this? " asked Huck.

" Sometimes; not always; not generally. I think we haven't got the right place."

So they chose a new spot and began again. The labour dragged a little, but still they made progress. Finally Huck leaned on his spade, wiped the sweat from his forehead with his sleeve and said:

" We must be in the wrong place again. What do you think? "

" It's very funny, Huck. I don't understand it. Oh, I know what the matter is! What fools we are! You must find out where the shadow of the limb falls at midnight, and that's where you dig! "

" Then, hang it all, we've done all this work for nothing. Now we've got to come back at night. It's a very long way. Well, I'll come round and meow to-night."

The boys were there that night about the appointed time. They sat in the shadow waiting. It was a lonely place and the boys talked little. Presently they judged that midnight had come. They marked where the shadow fell and began to dig hopefully. The hole deepened and deepened, but every time their hearts jumped when they heard the pick strike upon something, they only suffered a new disappointment. It was only a stone or a root.

" It's no use, Huck," said Tom at last. " We're wrong again."

" But we can't be wrong. We marked the shadow exactly."

" I know, but there's another thing. We only guessed

the time. Perhaps it was too late or too early."

Huck dropped his spade.

"That's it," he said. "We can never tell the right time, and besides, this kind of thing is too awful. I feel as if there is something horrible behind me all the time; and I'm afraid to turn round, because perhaps there are others in front waiting for a chance to jump at me. I've felt queer all over ever since I got here."

"Well, I've felt the same, Huck. They nearly always put in a dead man when they bury a treasure under a tree, to watch it."

"Good heavens!"

"Yes, they do. I've always heard that."

"Tom, I don't like to interfere with places where there are dead people. One's sure to get into trouble with them."

"I don't like to stir them up either, Huck. Suppose this one here was to stick his head out and say something!"

"Don't, Tom! It's awful! I say, let's give this place up and try somewhere else."

Tom considered for a moment, and then said:

"The haunted house! That's it!"

"I don't like haunted houses, Tom. Why, they're far worse than dead people. Dead people may talk, but they don't come sliding round in a sheet when you're not noticing and peep over your shoulder all of a sudden and grind their teeth the way a ghost does. I couldn't bear such a thing as that, Tom. Nobody could."

"Yes, but, Huck, ghosts only travel about at night. They won't hinder us from digging there in the daytime. So what's the use of being afraid?"

"Well, all right. We'll try the haunted house if you say so; but I think it's taking a risk."

They had started to go down the hill by this time. There in the middle of the moonlit valley stood the haunted house, utterly lonely, its fences gone long ago, weeds hiding the doorstep, the chimney in ruins, the window-frames without glass, a corner of the roof fallen in. The boys went far to the right, to keep as far as possible from such an evil-looking place.

CHAPTER 22

IN THE HAUNTED HOUSE

ABOUT noon the next day the boys arrived at the dead tree. They had come for their tools.

" I say, Tom, do you know what day it is?" said Huck suddenly.

Tom thought, and then said, with a startled look in his eyes, "Good heavens! I never once thought of it, Huck!"

"Well, I didn't either, but all at once I remembered that to-day is Friday."

"Hang it; one can't be too careful, Huck. We might have got into an awful lot of trouble, starting such a thing on a Friday."

"*Might!* Better say would! There are some lucky days, perhaps, but Friday isn't one of them."

So they gave up their search and played Robin Hood all the afternoon.

On Saturday, soon after midday, they were back at the dead tree again. They shouldered their tools and marched off.

When they reached the haunted house, the dead silence and the loneliness of the place were so repellent that they were afraid, for a moment, to go in. Then they crept inside. They saw a dusty room with an ancient fireplace, broken windows and a ruined stair-case. They talked in whispers, listening to catch the slightest sound and ready for an instant retreat.

After a time they became bolder, and gave the place

a critical and interested examination. Next they wanted to look upstairs. They threw their tools in a corner and made the ascent. They found the same signs of decay. They were about to go down and begin work when Tom whispered:

"*Sh!*"

"What is it?" asked Huck, going as white as a sheet with fright.

"*Sh!* There! Hear it?"

"Yes! Oh, let's run!"

"Keep still! Don't move! They're coming right towards the door."

The terrified boys stretched themselves upon the floor with their eyes to holes in the boards and lay waiting.

Two men entered. Each boy said to himself:

"There's the old deaf and dumb Spaniard who's been in the town once or twice lately. I've never seen the other man before."

The "other," who was talking in a low voice, was a ragged fellow with an unpleasant face. The Spaniard was wrapped in a big, loose overcoat. He had a bushy white beard, long white hair flowed from under his wide hat and he wore dark spectacles. They sat down on the floor and the "other" went on talking.

"No, I've thought it over and it's too dangerous."

"Dangerous!" repeated the "deaf and dumb" Spaniard, to the immense surprise and horror of the boys. They gasped and shivered. It was Redskin Joe's voice!

"Don't be a coward," continued Redskin Joe. "Isn't coming here in the daytime dangerous? Anyone who saw us would suspect us."

"I know that," replied the stranger, "but there isn't any other place as suitable. I want to leave this place. I wanted to yesterday, but it wasn't any use trying to move out with those accursed boys playing over there."

"Those accursed boys" shivered again. The two

men got out some food and ate in silence.

"Look here," said Redskin Joe after a time. "Go back to your home up the river. Wait there till you hear from me. I'll risk going into this town just once more, for a look round. We'll do that job, which you think is dangerous, after I've spied round a little and think everything's favourable. Then we'll set out for Texas together."

This seemed satisfactory. Both men soon began yawning and Redskin Joe said:

"I can hardly keep my eyes open. It's your turn to watch."

He curled up on the floor and was soon fast asleep. Presently the watcher began to nod and he, too, slept.

The boys drew a long, grateful breath. Tom whispered:

"Now's our chance! Come!"

Tom urged. Huck held back. At last Tom rose softly, but the first step he took produced such a terrible creak from the rotten floor that he sank down almost dead with fright. He did not make a second attempt.

As the sun was setting, Redskin Joe sat up, stared round and then stirred his companion with his foot.

"You're a fine watchman, aren't you?"

"It's all right, though. Nothing's happened."

"Well, it's nearly time to be moving, partner," said Redskin Joe. "What shall we do with that money we've got left?"

"I don't know," said the stranger. "Leave it here as we've always done. It's no use taking it away till we start south. Six hundred and fifty dollars in silver is a lot to carry."

"Yes, but it may be a long time before I get the right chance for that job. Accidents may happen, and it isn't in a very safe place. We'll bury it properly."

"Good idea," said Redskin Joe's companion, who walked across the room, raised one of the big flat stones in the fireplace and lifted out a bag. He took from it twenty or thirty dollars for himself and the same amount for Redskin Joe, and then passed it to the latter, who was on his knees in the corner now, digging with his knife.

The boys forgot all their fears, all their miseries in an instant. With wide eyes they watched every movement. Luck! This was better than anything they could have imagined. Here was the best kind of treasure-hunting, without any troublesome uncertainty as to where to dig.

The half-breed's knife struck something.

" Hello! " he exclaimed.

" What is it? " asked his companion.

" It's a box, I believe. Here, help me and we'll see what it's here for. Never mind, I've made a hole in it."

He put his hand in and drew it out.

" It's money! "

The two men examined the handful of coins. They were gold. The boys above were as excited as the men, and as delighted.

" There's an old, rusty pick in the corner," said the stranger. " I saw it a minute ago."

He ran and brought the boys' pick and spade. Redskin Joe took the pick, looked it over critically, shook his head, muttered something to himself and then began to use it. The box was soon unearthed.

" Partner, there are thousands of dollars here," said Redskin Joe.

" I've often heard that Murrel's gang was around here one summer," remarked the stranger. " This is probably their money. Well, now you won't need to do that job."

The half-breed frowned. A wicked light shone in his eyes. " You don't know me. It isn't robbery altogether. It's revenge! And I'll need your help in it."

" All right. What shall we do with this? Bury it again? "

" Yes." (The boys above were delighted.) " No!

No!'' (Deep disappointment above.) '' I'd nearly forgotten. That pick had fresh earth on it!'' (The boys were sick with terror in a moment.) '' Why are a pick and a spade here? Who brought them? Have you heard anybody? Seen anybody? What! Shall we bury it again and leave them to come and see the ground disturbed? Never! We'll take it to my place.''

'' Why, of course! You mean number one?''

'' No—number two—under the cross,'' replied Redskin Joe. '' Number one is not safe enough.''

'' All right. It's nearly dark enough to start.''

The half-breed got up and went about from window to window, cautiously peeping out.

'' Who could have brought those tools here?'' he asked presently. '' Do you think they can be upstairs?''

The boys' blood ran cold. Redskin Joe put his hand on his knife, stood for a moment undecided, and then turned towards the staircase. His steps came creaking up the stairs. Both the boys were shivering as if with a dozen fevers. Crash! Redskin Joe landed on the floor amidst the rotten wood of the fallen staircase. He picked himself up, cursing, and his companion said:

'' Now what's the use of that? If anybody's up there, let them stay there. Who cares? In my opinion, whoever left those tools here caught sight of us and thought we were devils or ghosts. I bet they're running yet.''

Redskin Joe muttered for some time. Soon afterwards they slipped out of the house in the deepening twilight and moved towards the river with their precious box.

Tom and Huck got up, weak but immensely relieved. They had not the slightest desire to follow Redskin Joe and the stranger. They were content to reach the ground without broken necks. They did not talk much on the way home. They were too busy hating themselves and the bad luck that made them take the tools there. But for that, Redskin Joe would never have suspected and would have left the silver and the gold. They determined to keep a look-out for that Spaniard when he came to town, spying out for chances to do his revengeful job and to follow him to "number two," wherever that might be.

CHAPTER 23

"TRACK THE MONEY!"

TOM had a fearful dream that night. As he lay next morning recalling the details, he noticed that they seemed curiously far away and unreal. Then it occurred to him that the great adventure itself must be a dream! This uncertainty must be swept away. He would have a hurried breakfast and find Huck.

Huck was sitting on the edge of a boat and looking very miserable.

"Hello, Huck!"

"Hello, Tom!"

Silence for a minute.

"Tom, if we'd left the tools at the dead tree, we'd have got the money. Oh, aren't we unlucky!"

"It's not a dream, then!"

"Dream! I've had horrible dreams all night, with that Spanish devil chasing us all through them, curse him!"

"Don't curse him. Find him! Track the money!"

"Tom, we'll never find him. And I'd be frightened to death if I did see him."

"Well, so would I; but I'd like to see him and track him—to his number two."

"Number two; yes, that's it. I've been thinking about that. But it's a mystery to me. What do you think it is?"

"I don't know. It's too difficult. I say, Huck, perhaps it's the number of a house!"

"No, Tom, that isn't it. If it is, it's not in this one-horse town. There aren't any numbers here."

"Well, that's so. Let me think a minute. I know! It's the number of a room—in an inn, I'm sure!"

"You've got it! There are only two inns. We can find out quickly."

"Wait here, Huck, till I come back."

Tom was off at once. He did not care to have Huck's company in public places. He was away half an hour. He found out that in the better inn number two had long been occupied by a young lawyer, and was still occupied. In the other inn, number two was a mystery. The innkeeper's young son said that it was kept locked all the time and that he never saw anybody go into it or come out of it except at night. He had noticed that there was a light in the room the night before and ex-plained the mystery by suggesting that it was haunted.

"That's what I've found out, Huck. I think that's the very number two we're after."

"I think it is, Tom. Now what are you going to do?"

"Let me think."

Tom thought for a long time. Then he said:

"I'll tell you. The back door of that number two is in the little lane behind the inn. Now you get all the doorkeys that you can find and I'll take auntie's, and the first dark night we'll go there and try them. And remember to keep a look-out for Redskin Joe, because he said he was going to spy round once more for a chance to get his revenge. If you see him, just follow him. If he doesn't go to that number two, that isn't the place!"

"Good heavens! I don't want to follow him by myself!"

"Why, it'll be night. He might never see you; and if he did, perhaps he'd never suspect anything."

"Well, if it's really dark, I'll follow him. Well—I don't know—I don't know. All right, I'll try."

"Believe me, I'll follow him if it's dark, Huck! Why, he might be going straight to that money!"

"That's so, Tom; that's so. I'll follow him. I will; I swear I will."

"Now that's the way to talk! Don't you ever weaken, Huck, and I won't."

So that night Tom and Huck waited about the neighbourhood of the inn until after nine, one watching the lane at a distance and the other the inn door. Nobody entered the lane or left it; nobody at all like the Spaniard entered or left the inn door. So Tom went home, having agreed that if the night was very dark, Huck was to come and meow; then Tom would slip out and try the keys. But the night was clear, and Huck ended his watch and retired to bed in an empty barrel about midnight.

On Tuesday the boys had the same bad luck, and on Wednesday also. However, Thursday night seemed more promising. Tom slipped out with his aunt's old tin lamp and a large towel to cover it with. He hid the lamp in Huck's barrel and the watch began. An hour before midnight the inn closed and its lights were put out. No Spaniard had been seen. Nobody had entered or left the lane. Everything was favourable. All was in darkness, and the perfect stillness was interrupted only by occasional mutterings of distant thunder.

Tom got his lamp, lit it in the barrel and wrapped it closely in the towel, and the two adventurers crept in the gloom towards the inn. Huck stood on guard and Tom felt his way into the lane. Huck was full of anxiety as he waited.

Suddenly there was a flash of light and Tom came flying past him.

"Run for your life!" he gasped. "Run for your life!"

He need not have repeated it; once was enough.

Huck was travelling thirty or forty miles an hour before the repetition was out of Tom's mouth. The boys did not stop till they reached a deserted shed at the lower end of the village. Just as they got inside the rain poured down. As soon as Tom got his breath he said:

"Huck, it was awful! I tried two of the keys just as softly as I could, but they wouldn't turn in the lock. Well, without noticing what I was doing I took hold of the door-handle, and the door came open! It wasn't locked! I crept in and shook off the towel, and then——"

"Go on! What happened, Tom?"

"Huck, I almost stepped on Redskin Joe's hand!"

"No!"

"Yes! He was lying there, fast asleep on the floor, with his arms spread out."

"Good heavens! What did you do? Did he wake up?"

"No, he never moved. Drunk, I think. I just snatched up that towel and ran."

"I'd never have thought of the towel."

"Well, I would. My aunt would skin me alive if I lost it."

"I say, Tom, did you see that box?"

"Huck, I didn't wait to look round. I didn't see the box. I didn't see the cross. I didn't see anything except a bottle and a tin cup on the floor beside Redskin Joe. Yes, and I saw two barrels and many more bottles in the room. Don't you see, now, what's wrong with that haunted room?"

"What?"

"Why, it's haunted with drink! They pretend they don't sell drink there."

"Who would have thought such a thing! But I say, Tom, now is a good time to get that box, if Redskin Joe's drunk."

"Is it? You try it!"

Huck shivered.

" Well, no; I don't think I will."

" And I think not, Huck. Only one bottle beside
Redskin Joe isn't enough. If there were three, I'd do
it."

There was a long pause for thought, and then Tom
said:

" Look here, Huck, let's not try any more until we
know Redskin Joe's not there. It's too frightful. If
we watch every night we'll be absolutely sure to see
him go out some time or other. Then we'll snatch that
box quicker than lightning."

" All right. I'll watch the whole night, and I'll do it
every night, too, if you'll do the other part of the job."

" I will. All you've got to do is to come round to
the house and meow, and if I'm asleep throw some
stones up at the window and that will bring me out.
Now, Huck, the storm's over and I'll go home. It'll
be daylight in a couple of hours. If I don't want you
in the daytime, Huck, I'll let you sleep. I won't come
round and worry you. If you see that something's
happening in the night, just come round and meow."

CHAPTER 24

THE PICNIC: HUCK ON THE TRACK

THE first thing Tom heard on Friday morning was a
glad piece of news; Judge Thatcher's family had come
back to town. He saw Becky with a crowd of their
schoolmates and his delight was boundless when she
told him that her mother had appointed the next day
for the long-delayed picnic. Invitations were sent out
before sunset. Tom had hopes of hearing Huck's meow
and of astonishing Becky and the picnickers with the
treasure the next day, but no signal came.

By ten o'clock the next morning a gay company had
gathered at Judge Thatcher's, and everything was

ready for a start. The children were put in charge of
a few young teachers of the Sunday-school. The ferryboat had been hired for the occasion. Soon the joyful
crowd carrying baskets of food hurried up the main
street. The last thing Mrs. Thatcher said to Becky
was:

" You'll not get back till late, child. Perhaps you'd
better stay all night with some of the girls who live near
the ferry-landing."

"Then I'll stay with Susie Harper, mamma," said
Becky.

As Tom and Becky hurried along, Tom said:

" I say, I'll tell you what we'll do. Instead of going
to Mrs. Harper's we'll climb right up the hill and stay
at Widow Douglas's. She'll have lovely cakes! And
she'll be so glad to have us!"

" But what will mamma say?" said Becky hesitatingly.

However, the Widow Douglas's kind heart and
Tom's persuasions tempted Becky and it was decided
to say nothing to anybody about their new programme.

Soon it occurred to Tom that Huck might give the
signal this very night; but the signal did not come the
night before, so why should it be any more likely to
come to-night? He determined not to allow himself to
think of the box of money another time that day.

Three miles below the town the ferryboat was tied
up at the mouth of a little wooded valley. The crowd
swarmed ashore. Games were arranged and soon the
forest echoed far and wide with shouting and laughter
Then came the destruction of the good things in their
baskets. After the feast there was a refreshing rest and
talk in the shade. Presently somebody shouted:

" Who's ready for the cave?"

Everybody was. Bundles of candles were produced
and at once everyone began to climb up the hill. The
mouth of the cave was high up the hillside. Its massive
door stood unbarred. Inside was a small chamber, as

cold as an ice-chest and walled by Nature with solid limestone. Candles were lit and the children made their way down the steep descent of the main path, which was not more than eight or ten feet wide. The candle-light dimly revealed the arched roof overhead. Every few steps other narrower passages branched off on either hand, for the cave contained a very great number of twisting passages. No one knew the end of it. Most of the young men of the village knew a small part of it, and it was not customary to go beyond this.

The procession moved along the main avenue for about three-quarters of a mile, and then children began to slip aside into branch passages and play hide-and-seek, taking each other by surprise where the passages joined again. Finally one group after another came wandering back, breathless, covered with clay and candle-drippings from head to foot, and entirely delighted with the success of the day. They were astonished to find that the sun had set. The bell had been calling for half an hour. When the ferryboat with her merry passengers pushed into the river, nobody cared a straw for the wasted time but the captain.

Huck was already watching when the ferryboat's lights went glittering past. He heard no noise on board, for the children were as quiet as people who are tired out usually are. The night was growing cloudy and dark. Eleven o'clock came and the inn lights were put out. Huck waited a weary long time, but nothing happened. Why not give it up and go to bed?

A noise reached his ear. He sprang into a doorway. The next moment two men brushed by him, and one seemed to have something under his arm. It must be that box! So they were going to remove the treasure. Should he call Tom now? No, that would be silly; the men would get away and never be found again. He must follow.

They walked a short distance up the street leading

to the river and turned to the left up a cross-street. Then they went straight ahead until they came to the path that led up Cardiff Hill. This they took. Halfway up the hill they passed the house of the old Welshman, Mr. Jones, and still climbed upward among the tall bushes. Huck shortened his distance now, for they would never be able to see him. He hurried on for a time and then slowed down, fearing that he was getting too near them. He stopped and listened. He was about to spring on when a man cleared his throat not four feet from him! Huck's heart shot into his mouth, but he swallowed it again. He knew where he was, within five steps of the fence around Widow Douglas's grounds.

Now there was a very low voice; Redskin Joe's.

"Curse her. Perhaps she has guests. There are lights, although it's late."

"Yes, there must be guests there. Better give it up, then." This was the voice of the stranger of the haunted house.

"Give it up, just when I'm about to leave this country for ever? Never! I tell you again, I don't want her money. But her husband was the Judge who had me thrown into prison as a vagabond. And that isn't the millionth part of it! He had me horsewhipped, horsewhipped like a slave, with all the town looking on! He died, and escaped me. But she'll suffer for it!"

"Oh, don't kill her! Don't do that!"

"Kill? Who said anything about killing? When you want to take revenge on a pretty woman, you don't kill her. No! You go for her face, and spoil it with a knife!"

"My God! That's——"

"Keep your opinion to yourself! My friend, you'll help me. If you hesitate, I'll kill you! Do you understand that? And if I have to kill you, I'll kill her, and then nobody will know who did the job."

"Well, the quicker we do it the better."

" Now? And people there? No, we'll wait until the lights are out. There's no hurry."

With infinite care Huck stepped back little by little, until he judged that he was safe. Then he flew like the wind. Down, down he raced till he reached the Welshman's. He banged at the door and the heads of the old man and his sons were thrust from windows.

" Let me in, Mr. Jones! Quick! It's Huckleberry Finn! I'll tell you everything!"

" Let him in, boys, and let's see what the trouble is."

" Please don't tell anyone that I told you," were Huck's first words when he got in. " Please don't; I'd be killed. But the widow's been a good friend to me sometimes, and I want to tell."

" He must have something important to tell us, or he wouldn't behave so," said the old man. " Speak out, Huck. I promise you that nobody here will ever tell."

Huck hurriedly told them what he had overheard, and a few minutes later the old man and his sons, well armed, were up the hill and tiptoeing towards the fence. Huck, hidden behind a great rock, listened anxiously. All of a sudden there was the sound of shots and a cry. Huck waited for no details. He dashed down the hill as fast as his legs could carry him.

CHAPTER 25

HUCK QUESTIONED: TOM AND BECKY MISSING

BEFORE sunrise on Sunday morning Huck tapped at the old Welshman's door. A call came from a window:

" Who's there?"

" Only Huck Finn."

" That's a name that can open this door night or day. Welcome!"

These were strange words to the ears of the vagabond

boy, and the pleasantest he had ever heard. The door was quickly unlocked and the old man and his sons speedily dressed themselves.

"Now, my boy, I hope you're hungry, because breakfast will soon be ready. The boys and I hoped that you would stay here last night."

"I was terrified," said Huck, "and I ran three miles without stopping. I've come now because I want to know about it; and I've come before daylight because I didn't want to come across those devils, even if they were dead."

"No, they're not dead, Huck. We fired at them, but they got away in the dark. Then we put the police on their tracks. A description of the scoundrels would help a great deal. Did you see what they were like?"

"Yes, one's the deaf and dumb Spaniard that's been around here once or twice, and the other is a nasty-looking, ragged——"

"The deaf and dumb Spaniard talking? Well, never mind now. We know the men. I came across them in the woods at the back of the widow's house one day, and they crept away. Off you go, boys, and tell the Sheriff!"

As the Welshman's sons were leaving the room, Huck sprang up and cried:

"Oh, please don't tell anybody that I told you about them! Oh, please!"

"My boy, don't be afraid of me. I wouldn't hurt a hair of your head for the world. No, I'd protect you. Why are you so frightened of these men? What do you know about them? That Spaniard is not deaf and dumb. Do you know who he is? Now trust me. I won't betray you."

Huck looked into the old man's honest eyes for a moment, and then bent over and whispered in his ear:

"It isn't a Spaniard! It's Redskin Joe in disguise!"

The old Welshman almost jumped out of his chair.

" It's all plain enough now. When you told me of that knife business, I judged that it was your own fancy, because Spaniards don't take that sort of revenge."

During breakfast the talk went on. The old man said that before going to bed he and his sons had got a lamp and had examined the place near the fence for signs of blood. They found nothing but a bundle of——

" Of what? "

The words had leapt to Huck's lips. He waited breathlessly for an answer.

The Welshman started, stared in return, then replied:

" Thieves' tools."

Huck sank back, infinitely grateful.

The Welshman eyed him curiously, and then said:

" What were you expecting we'd found? "

Huck did not know what excuse to make. Then a senseless reply came into his head. There was no time to consider it, so he said weakly:

" Sunday-school books, perhaps."

The old man roared with laughter, but poor Huck was too troubled to smile.

" Poor fellow, you look pale," said the old man. " You're not well. I'm not surprised that you're a bit queer. Rest and sleep are what you need."

Huck was annoyed to think that he had been such a fool and betrayed such a suspicious excitement.

Just as breakfast was over, there was a knock at the door. Huck quickly hid, for he had no desire to be connected with the events of the previous night. The Welshman admitted several ladies and gentlemen, among them the Widow Douglas. The Welshman had to tell the story of the night to the visitors. The widow expressed her deep gratitude for her preservation.

" Don't thank me, madam. But for another, who won't allow me to give his name, my boys and I would never have been there."

Of course this aroused the great curiosity of the visitors, who later spread it in the town, for the old man refused to reveal his secret.

There was no Sunday-school during the holidays, but everybody was early at church and the stirring happenings on Cardiff Hill were thoroughly discussed. News came that not a sign of the villains had yet been discovered. When the service was finished Judge Thatcher's wife came up to Mrs. Harper as she was moving down the church with the crowd, and said:

"Is my Becky going to sleep all day? I expected that she would be tired out."

"Your Becky?"

"Yes," with a startled look. "Didn't she stay with you last night?"

"Why, no!"

Mrs. Thatcher turned pale, and sank into a seat just as Aunt Polly, talking with a friend, passed by. Aunt Polly said:

"Good morning, Mrs. Thatcher. Good morning, Mrs. Harper. Tom's missing. He stayed with one of you last night, I expect, and now he's afraid to come to church."

Mrs. Thatcher shook her head weakly and turned paler than ever.

"He didn't stay with us," said Mrs. Harper, beginning to look uneasy. An anxious expression came into Aunt Polly's face.

Children were questioned, and the Sunday-school teachers. They all said that they had not noticed whether Tom and Becky were on the ferryboat on the homeward trip. No one had thought of inquiring whether anyone was missing. One young man thoughtlessly expressed his fear that they were still in the cave! Mrs. Thatcher fainted away. Aunt Polly started weeping.

The alarm swept from street to street. Within five minutes the bells of the church were ringing wildly. Horses were saddled. The ferryboat was ordered out. In half an hour two hundred men were pouring down the main road and the river towards the cave.

All the long afternoon the village seemed dead. All the wearisome night the town waited anxiously for news; but when the morning came at last, the only message from the cave was: "Send more candles and food." Mrs. Thatcher was almost mad with grief, and Aunt Polly also.

The old Welshman came home towards midnight, almost worn out. He found Huck in bed with a raging fever. The doctors were all at the cave, so the Widow Douglas took charge of the patient. She said that she would do her best for him, whether he was good or bad, because no human being should be neglected.

Before midday parties of exhausted men returned to the village, but the strongest villagers continued searching. All the news that could be gained was that the depths of the cave were being examined; that wherever one wandered through the passages lights could be seen and shouts and pistol-shots heard; that the names "BECKY" and "TOM," done in candle-smoke, had been found on a rocky wall far from the part usually visited by tourists.

Three dreadful days and nights dragged by, and the village sank into despair.

CHAPTER 26

LOST IN THE CAVE

Now to return to the share of Tom and Becky in the picnic. They danced along the passages with the rest of the children, visiting the familiar wonders of the cave, such as "Aladdin's Palace" and "The Castle

Hall." When the game of hide-and-seek began, Tom and Becky played until they lost interest in it. Then they wandered down winding passages, holding their candles up and reading the network of names, dates and addresses done in candle-smoke on the rocky walls. They went on and on, smoked their own names under an overhanging shelf and proceeded.

Presently they came to a place where a little stream of water had, throughout the centuries, formed a filmy waterfall in sparkling stone. Tom pressed his small body behind it to light it up for Becky, and found that it hid a sort of steep, natural stairway enclosed between narrow walls. At once the ambition to be a discoverer seized him. They made a smoke mark for future guidance and wound this way and that, far down into the depths of the cave. In one place they found a wide hall, from the roof of which hung a great number of shining white pillars of stone. After wondering and admiring, they left it by one of the numerous passages that opened into it. This soon brought them to a lovely spring, the basin of which seemed to be decorated with sparkling diamonds. It was in the midst of a cave where great columns rose from the floor to meet those from the roof; some had already joined. The children marvelled at this result of the ceaseless water-drip of centuries. Under the roof bats[1] had packed themselves together, thousands in a bunch, and they came flocking down in hundreds, dashing furiously at the candles. Tom seized Becky's hand and hurried her into the first passage they came to, and by turning into every new passage they met they at last got rid of the troublesome creatures. Then Tom found an underground lake. which stretched away until its shape was lost in the shadows. He wanted to explore its borders, but decided that it would be best to sit down and rest for a time. Now for the first time the stillness of the place laid its damp and cold hand upon the minds of the

[1] A bat=a creature like a mouse with wings.

children.

"I wonder how long we've been down here, Tom?" said Becky. "We'd better go back."

"Yes, I think we'd better."

"Can you find the way, Tom? It's all mixed up to me."

"I think I can find it, but the bats—— If they put out both our candles we'll be in an awful difficulty. Let's try some other way."

They started off along a passage, looking at each new opening to see if there was anything familiar about it; but they were all strange.

"Oh, Tom, never mind the bats!" said Becky at last. "Let's go back that way. We seem to get worse and worse all the time."

Tom stopped.

"Listen!" said he.

The silence was so deep that even their own breathing seemed loud. Tom shouted. The shout went echoing down the empty avenues, and died out in the distance in a faint sound that was just like mocking laughter.

"Oh, don't do it again, Tom; it's too horrid," said Becky.

"It is horrid, but I'd better, Becky; they *might* hear us, you know," and he shouted again.

The "might" was even a greater horror than the ghostly laughter; it confessed that hope was dying. They listened; but there was no result. Tom turned back, but soon a certain indecision in his manner revealed another fearful fact to Becky; he could not find his way back.

"Oh, Tom, you didn't make any marks!"

"Becky, I was a fool. No, I can't find the way. It's all mixed up."

"Tom, Tom, we're lost! We're lost! We can never, never get out of this awful place! Oh, why did we leave the others!"

She sank to the ground and burst into such a dreadful storm of tears that Tom feared that she might go mad. When her weeping became a little less violent, he begged her not to give up hope. Then he began blaming himself. She told him not to talk like that again, for she was as much to blame as he was, she said.

So they moved on, aimlessly, for all they could do was to keep moving.

After a time Tom took Becky's candle and blew it out. Words were not needed. She knew that Tom had a whole candle and three or four pieces in his pocket, yet he must use as little as possible.

Then the children began to feel weary, but they tried to pay no attention. Moving was at least progress and might have a good result, but to sit down was to invite certain death.

At last Becky's weak limbs refused to carry her any farther. They sat down. They talked of home, of the friends there, and, above all, of the sunlight. Weariness weighed so heavily on Becky that she fell asleep, and Tom was grateful. He sat lost in thought of happier times.

When Becky woke up, she gave a gay little laugh, but she stopped it suddenly, and a groan followed.

"Oh, how *could* I sleep! I wish I had never woke! No, no, Tom, I don't! Don't look so! I won't say that again."

They rose and wandered along, hand in hand and hopeless. A long time after this Tom said that they must go quietly and listen for dripping water, because they must find a spring. They found one, and Tom said that they must rest again. Both were cruelly tired, yet Becky thought that she could go on a little farther. She was surprised to hear Tom disagree. Nothing was said for some time. Then Becky broke the silence:

"Tom, I am so hungry!"

Tom took a big cake from his pocket and divided it,

and Becky ate with good appetite. Tom pretended to eat his share. There was an abundance of cold water with which to finish the food. Soon Becky suggested that they should move on again. Tom was silent, and then he said:

" Becky, we must stay here, where there's water to drink. This little piece of candle is our last ! "

Becky cried again. At length she said:

" Tom ! "

" Well, Becky ? "

" They'll miss us and search for us ! Perhaps they're searching for us now ! "

" Why, of course they are ! "

" When would they miss us, Tom ? "

" When they got back to the boat, I suppose."

" Tom, it might have been dark then. Would they notice that we hadn't come ? "

" I don't know. Anyway, your mother would miss you as soon as they all got home."

A frightened look in Becky's face made Tom remember. She was not to have gone home that night ! The Sunday morning might be half spent before Mrs. Thatcher discovered that Becky was not at Mrs. Harper's. In a moment a new burst of grief from Becky showed Tom that the thought in his mind had struck hers also.

The children fastened their eyes upon the bit of candle and watched it melt slowly and pitilessly away. They saw the little flame rise and fall, rise and fall, and then, suddenly, the horror of utter darkness enveloped them.

How long afterwards it was that Becky woke to find herself crying in Tom's arms, neither could tell. Tom said that it might be Sunday, or perhaps Monday. The hours crawled by, and again the captives felt faint with hunger. Tom's share of the cake was divided and eaten, but it seemed to leave them hungrier than before.

Presently Tom said:

"*Sh!* Did you hear that?"

Both held their breath and listened. There was a sound like the faintest far-off shout. Instantly Tom answered it. Again the sound was heard, and apparently a little nearer.

"They're coming! Come along, Becky! We're all right now!"

The joy of the prisoners was almost unbearable. Their speed was slow, however, because pits were rather common, and had to be guarded against. They soon came to one. Tom lay flat and reached down, but he could not touch the bottom. It might be three feet deep, it might be a hundred. They must stay there until the searchers came. They listened. The distant shoutings were growing more distant! A moment or two more, and they had gone altogether. The heart-breaking misery of it! Tom shouted until his throat ached, but it was of no use. He talked hopefully to Becky, but a long time passed and no sound came.

The children felt their way back to the spring. The time dragged on. They slept again, and awoke hungry and miserable.

Now Tom had an idea. It would be better to explore some of the side passages than to remain idle. He took his kite-string from his pocket, tied one end to a big stone and started with Becky, unwinding the line as they crawled along. At the end of twenty steps the passage ended in a pit. Tom felt below and then as far round the corner as he could. At that moment a hand, holding a candle, appeared from behind a rock! Tom gave a glad shout and instantly that hand was followed by the body it belonged to—Redskin Joe's! Tom was turned to stone. To his immense relief the "Spaniard" fled. Tom told Becky that he had only shouted "for luck," and they crept back to the spring.

But hunger and misery after a time make one forget one's fears. Another wearisome wait and another long sleep brought changes. The children awoke, sick with hunger. Tom believed that it must be Wednesday or Thursday, or even Friday or Saturday now. He proposed to explore another passage. He felt willing to risk Redskin Joe and all other terrors. But Becky was so weak that she could not be roused. She said that she could wait, now, where she was, and die; it would not be long. She told Tom to explore if he chose, but she begged him to come back from time to time and speak to her. She made him promise that when her last hour came, he would stay by her and hold her hand until all was over. With a lump in his throat, Tom pretended to be confident of finding the searchers or a way out of the cave, and with the kite-string in his hand went crawling down one of the passages, sick with hunger and sorrow and visions of their coming fate.

CHAPTER 27

SAVED

TUESDAY afternoon came. The village of St. Petersburg still mourned. Public prayers had been said for the lost children. Most of the searchers had given up the task and had gone back to their daily work, saying that it was plain that the children could never be found. Mrs. Thatcher was very ill, and most of the time her mind was wandering. People said that it was heartbreaking to hear her call her child and see her raise her head and listen. Aunt Polly's grey hair had grown almost white. The village went sadly to its rest on Tuesday night.

In the middle of the night a wild burst of ringing broke from the village bells, and in a moment the streets were swarming with excited, half-dressed people who shouted, "Get up! Get up! They're found! They're found!" The beating of tin pans and the blowing of horns added to the uproar. The crowd moved towards the river, met the children coming in an open carriage drawn by shouting villagers, gathered round it, joined its homeward march and swept gloriously up the main street, cheering madly !

The village was lit up; nobody went to bed again; it was the greatest night the little town had ever seen. During the first half-hour a procession of villagers made their way one by one through Judge Thatcher's house, seized the saved ones and kissed them, shook Mrs. Thatcher's hand and wandered out, raining tears all over the place.

Aunt Polly's happiness was complete and Mrs. Thatcher's nearly so. It would be complete as soon as the messenger sent to the cave with the great news reached her husband.

Tom lay on a couch with an eager audience about him and told the history of the wonderful adventure, closing with a description of their escape. He followed two passages as far as his kite-string would reach; he followed a third to the end of the string, and was about to turn back when he caught sight of a far-off glimmer that looked like daylight; he crawled towards it, pushed his head and shoulders through a small hole and saw the broad Mississippi rolling by ! And if it had happened to be night he would not have seen that glimmer of daylight and would not have explored that passage any farther ! He told how he went back, broke the good news to Becky and managed to convince her. She almost died of joy when she saw the daylight. They pushed their way out and sat and cried with gladness. Some men came along in a boat and did not believe Tom's wild tale at first, " because," they said, " you are five miles down the river below the valley where the cave is." The boatmen rowed them to a house, gave them supper, made them rest till two or three hours after dark, and then brought them home.

Before daylight Judge Thatcher and the handful of searchers with him were informed of the great news.

The effects of three days and nights of exhaustion and hunger could not be shaken off at once, as Tom and Becky soon discovered. They had to stay in bed all Wednesday and Thursday. Tom was nearly as strong as ever by Saturday, but Becky did not leave her room until Sunday, and then she looked as if she had had a long illness.

Tom learned of Huck's sickness and went to see him. The Widow Douglas stayed by to see that no exciting subject was mentioned to the patient. At home Tom was told of the Cardiff Hill affair and that the ragged man's body had been found in the river near the ferry-landing. Perhaps he had been drowned while trying to escape.

A fortnight later, when Tom called at Judge Thatcher's to see Becky, the Judge and some friends made Tom talk. Someone asked him jokingly if he would like to go to the cave again. Tom said that he would not mind.

"Well, I've not the least doubt that there are others like you, Tom," said the Judge. "But we've prevented that. Nobody will get lost in that cave again."

"Why?"

"Because two weeks ago I had its big door strengthened and locks put on it, and I've got the keys."

Tom turned as white as a sheet.

"Oh, Judge, Redskin Joe's in the cave!"

CHAPTER 28

THE TREASURE FOUND

WITHIN a few minutes the news had spread and a dozen boats full of men were on their way to the cave, and the ferryboat well filled with passengers soon followed. Tom was in Judge Thatcher's boat.

When the cave door was unlocked, a sorrowful sight

presented itself. Redskin Joe lay stretched upon the ground, dead. He had died of hunger. His face was close to the crack of the door as if his longing eyes had been fixed to the last moment upon the light of the free world outside. Usually one could find half a dozen bits of candle stuck by tourists in the cracks of the walls of the first chamber, but now there were none. The prisoner had searched for them and eaten them. He had also managed to catch a few bats, and these also he had eaten, leaving only their claws.

Tom was sorry for him, for he knew from his own experience how this unfortunate man had suffered; but although he pitied him, it was a great relief to the boy to feel safe again.

Redskin Joe was buried near the mouth of the cave.

The morning after the funeral Tom took Huck aside to have an important talk. Huck had learned all about Tom's adventures from the Welshman and the Widow Douglas by this time. Huck described his entire adventure on Cardiff Hill, for Tom had only heard the Welshman's part of it.

"Well," said Huck finally, "I expect that the money in the box has gone from number two. It'll never be ours, Tom."

"Huck, that money never was in number two at the inn!"

"What!" Huck gazed keenly at his companion. "Tom, have you got on the track of it again?"

"Huck, it's in the cave!"

Huck's eyes blazed.

"Say that again, Tom!"

"The money's in the cave! Will you go with me and get it out?"

"Of course I will! But what makes you think that the money is——"

"Huck, just wait until we get there. If we don't find it, I'll give you everything I've got in the world."

"Is it far in the cave? I've been on my legs a

few days, but I don't think I could walk more than a mile."

"Huck, I'll take you there and back in a boat, and you needn't raise a finger."

"Let's start now, Tom."

"All right. We want some bread and meat, and our pipes, and a few bags, and two or three kite-strings, and some of those new things they call matches."

At noon the boys set out in a boat borrowed from a villager who was absent. When they were several miles below Cave Valley Tom said:

"Can you see that white place up there, where there's been a landslide? Well, that's where the hole is."

They landed, and Tom proudly marched into some thick bushes and said:

"Here it is! The finest hole in the country! I've always wanted to be a robber, but I knew I had to have something like this first. We'll keep it a secret, and tell only Joe Harper and Ben Rogers, because of course there must be a gang, for style. Tom Sawyer's Gang! It sounds splendid, doesn't it, Huck?"

"It does, Tom. And whom shall we rob?"

"Oh, almost anybody. We'll lie in wait for people, as robbers usually do."

"And kill them."

"No; not always. We'll hide them in the cave till they can pay a ransom."

"What's a ransom?"

"Money. You make them get all they can from their friends, and after you've kept them a year you kill them, if they haven't collected the money. Only you don't kill the women. They're always beautiful and rich and frightened to death. You take their watches and jewellery, but you always take your hat off and talk politely. Robbers are perfect gentlemen; you'll see that in any book."

"Why, it's grand, Tom! I believe it's even better

than being a pirate."

"Yes, it's better in some ways, because it's close to home and circuses and things."

The boys then entered the hole, Tom leading. They crawled to the farther end of the passage, made their kite-strings fast and moved on. They presently entered and followed Tom's other passage until they reached the pit. The candles revealed that it was only a steep clay slope, twenty or thirty feet deep.

Tom held up his candle and said:

"Look as far round that corner as you can. Do you see that? There, on the big rock over there, done with candle-smoke."

"Tom, it's a *cross* ! "

"Now we've found the real number two at last ! *'Under the cross,'* eh? That's just where I saw Redskin Joe hold up his candle ! "

Huck stared at the mysterious sign for a time, and then said in a shaky voice:

"Tom, let's get out of here ! "

"What ! And leave the treasure?"

"Yes, leave it. Redskin Joe's ghost is hanging about there, I'm certain."

"No, it isn't, Huck. It would haunt the place where he died, at the mouth of the cave, five miles from here."

"No, Tom, it wouldn't. It would hang round the money. I know the ways of ghosts, and so do you."

Doubts gathered in Tom's mind. Then an idea occurred to him.

"Look here, Huck, what fools we're making of ourselves ! Redskin Joe's ghost won't come where there's a cross ! "

"Tom, I didn't think of that. That's lucky for us. Let's hunt for that box."

Tom went first, cutting rough steps in the clay slope as he descended. Huck followed. Four passages opened out of the small cave in which the great rock stood. The boys examined them with no result. They found a corner in the one nearest the base of the rock with some blankets spread in it. But there was no money-box. They searched and re-searched this place, but in vain.

"He said *under* the cross," said Tom. "Well, the rock is under the cross, and the money can't be under the rock itself, because that's resting solidly on the ground."

They sat down discouraged. Huck could suggest nothing.

"Look here, Huck," said Tom at last; "there are footprints and some candle-grease on the clay about one side of this rock, but not on the other sides. Now, what does that mean? I bet you the money *is* under the rock. I'm going to dig in the clay."

"That's not a bad idea, Tom!" said Huck, brightening up.

Tom's knife was out at once and he had not dug four inches before he struck wood. Some boards were soon uncovered and removed. They had hidden a natural hole which led under the rock. Tom got into this and held his candle as far under the rock as he could, but said that he could not see the end. He proposed to explore. He bent down and passed under. The narrow way descended gradually. He followed its winding course with Huck at his heels. Tom suddenly turned a short curve and then exclaimed:

"Good heavens! Huck, look there!"

It was indeed the treasure-box, occupying a little cave. Near it were a couple of guns in leather cases, an empty powder-barrel, two or three pairs of old boots, a leather belt and some other rubbish.

"We've got it at last!" said Huck, digging among the coins with his hands. "We're rich, Tom!"

"Huck, it's too good to believe! Let me see if I can lift it."

The box weighed about fifty pounds. Tom could lift it in an awkward fashion, but he could not carry it conveniently.

"I thought so," he said. "It seemed heavy that day they carried it at the haunted house. It is a good thing that I brought the bags."

The money was soon in the bags, and the boys took it up to the cross rock.

"Now let's fetch the guns and things," said Huck.

"No, Huck, leave them there. They're just the things to have when we go robbing. We'll keep them there all the time, and hold our meetings there, too."

They soon came out into the bushes, and lunched and smoked in the boat. Tom rowed back in the long twilight and they landed a little after dark.

"Now, Huck," said Tom, "we'll hide the money in the widow's woodshed, and I'll come up in the morning and we'll count and divide. Then we'll hunt for a safe hiding-place for it out in the woods. Stay here while I borrow Benny Taylor's handcart. I won't be a minute."

He disappeared and presently returned with the handcart. They put the small sacks into it and started off, dragging the load behind them. When they reached the Welshman's house, they stopped to rest. Just as they were about to move on, the Welshman stepped out and said:

"Hello! Who's that?"

"Huck and Tom Sawyer."

"Good! Come along with me, boys; you're keeping everybody waiting. I'll pull the cart for you. Why, it's fairly heavy! What have you got in it? Bricks or old metal?"

"Old metal," said Tom.

The boys wanted to know why they had to hurry.

"Never mind. You'll see when we get to Widow Douglas's."

Mr. Jones left the cart near the door, and Huck and Tom found themselves pushed into Mrs. Douglas's sitting-room. The place was grandly lighted, and everybody that was of any importance in the village was there. The widow greeted them pleasantly, but Aunt Polly blushed with shame at their dirty condition and shook her head at Tom.

" I met them right at my door, and so I just brought them along in a hurry," said Mr. Jones.

" And you did right," said the widow. " Come with me, boys."

She took them to a bedroom, and said:

" Now wash and dress yourselves. Here are two new suits of clothes, shirts, socks, everything. They're Huck's—no, no thanks, Huck—Mr. Jones bought one and I bought the other. But they'll fit both of you. Put them on. We'll wait. Come down when you look respectable."

As she left, Sid appeared.

" Tom, auntie has been waiting for you all the afternoon."

" Why are all these people here?" asked Tom.

" It's one of the parties that the widow is always having. This time it's for the Welshman and his sons for saving her the other night."

Some minutes later the widow's guests, including a dozen children, were at the supper-table. At the proper time Mr. Jones made his little speech. He thanked the widow for the honour she was doing him and his sons, but said that there was another person who had played an important part in saving her. He then revealed the secret about Huck's share in the adventure. The widow heaped thanks and praise upon Huck, who, already suffering from the discomfort of his new clothes, had now to suffer a greater discomfort, the gaze and applause of everyone.

The widow said that her house was now Huck's home, that she meant to have him educated, and that when she could spare the money she would start him in business in a modest way. Tom's chance had come.

He said:

"Huck doesn't need it. He's rich!"

The silence was a little awkward. Tom broke it.

"Huck's got lots of money. Oh, you needn't smile. I can show you. Just wait a minute."

Tom ran outside. The guests looked at each other, puzzled, and inquiringly at Huck, who was tongue-tied.

Tom entered, struggling with his sacks. He poured the mass of yellow coin upon the table and said:

"There! What did I tell you? Half of it is Huck's, and half's mine."

The spectacle took everyone's breath away. Then there was a call for an explanation. Tom provided it, and there was scarcely an interruption from anyone to break the charm of its flow.

The money was counted. The sum amounted to a little over twelve thousand dollars. It was more than anyone present had ever seen before at one time, though several persons were there who were worth considerably more than that in property.

CHAPTER 29

HUCK "CAN'T BEAR THOSE WAYS"

THE boys' find caused great excitement in the poor little village of St. Petersburg. Every "haunted" house in St. Petersburg and the neighbouring villages was dug up for hidden treasure, and not by boys, but by men; some of them were serious, sensible men, too. Wherever Tom and Huck appeared they were admired and stared at. They were unable to remember that their remarks had possessed weight before, but now their sayings were treasured and repeated. Even the village paper published accounts of their lives.

The Widow Douglas invested[1] Huck's money at six per cent, and Judge Thatcher did the same with Tom's at Aunt Polly's request. Each boy had an income now that was simply gigantic, a dollar for every week-day in the year and half of the Sundays. For a dollar and a quarter a week in those simple days a boy could be fed, lodged and sent to school, and clothed and washed, too.

Judge Thatcher had formed a high opinion of Tom and said that he hoped to see him a great lawyer or a great soldier some day. He said that he meant to arrange that Tom should be admitted to the Military College and afterwards to the best law-school in the country, in order that he might be ready for either profession, or both.

Huck Finn's wealth, and the fact that he was under the Widow Douglas's protection, introduced him—no, dragged him—into society, and his sufferings were more than he could bear.

He bravely bore his miseries for three weeks, and then was missing. The widow was full of anxiety and searched for him everywhere. The public also searched high and low, and even dragged the river for his body. Early the third morning Tom wisely went hunting about among some old empty barrels behind a ruined shed, and in one of them he found the deserter. Huck had slept there. He had just breakfasted upon some stolen odds and ends, and was stretched out in comfort, smoking his pipe. He was untidy, uncombed, and dressed in the same old rags which he wore in the days when he was free and happy. Tom pulled him out, told him of the trouble he had been causing and urged him to go home. Huck's face lost its contentment.

" Don't talk about it, Tom," he said. " I've tried it, and it doesn't work. I'm not used to it. The widow's good to me, and friendly; but I can't bear those ways. She makes me get up at the same time

---

[1] To invest = to loan money in return for interest.

every morning. She makes me wash, and the servants comb me to pieces. She won't let me sleep in the wood-shed. I'm forced to wear those horrible clothes; they won't let any air get through, somehow, and while I'm wearing them I can't sit down, or lie down, or roll about anywhere. I have to go to church and wear shoes all Sunday. The widow gets up by a bell; she eats by a bell; she goes to bed by a bell. Everything's so horribly regular that I can't bear it."

"Well, everybody lives like that, Huck."

"Tom, I'm not everybody, and I can't bear it. It's awful to be tied up so. And food comes too easily; I don't take any interest in it that way. I have to ask to go fishing; I have to ask to go swimming; I have to ask if I want to do anything at all. They made me talk so nicely and correctly that I had to go in the woodshed and curse for a time to take the rotten taste out of my mouth, or I'd have died, Tom. The widow wouldn't let me smoke, she wouldn't let me shout, she wouldn't let me yawn, or stretch, or scratch in front of people. Besides, that school will be open soon, and she'd want me to go to it. I couldn't face that, Tom. Look here. Tom, being rich isn't what people pretend it is. It's only worry and worry, and sweat and sweat, and wish-ing all the time you were dead. Now these clothes suit me, and this barrel suits me, and I'm not going to leave them any more. Tom, that money has been the cause of all this trouble I'm in. Now take my share of it, give me a few cents now and again—not often, for I don't care much for a thing unless it's fairly hard to get —and beg the widow to let me go."

"Oh, Huck, you know I can't do that. It isn't fair, and besides, if you try this kind of life just a little longer, you'll begin to like it."

"Like it! Yes, you'll say next that I'd like a hot stove if I sat on it long enough! No, Tom, I won't be rich, and I won't be shut up in those horrible houses. I like the woods, and the river, and barrels, and I'll stick to them, too. Hang it! Just as we've got guns, and a cave, and are all ready to rob, the widow's foolishness spoils it all!''

Tom saw his opportunity.

"Look here, Huck, being rich isn't going to prevent me from being a robber.''

"No! Oh, do you really mean that, Tom?''

"It's as true as I'm sitting here. But, Huck, we can't let you join the gang if you're not respectable, you know.''

Huck's face clouded.

"You can't let me join, Tom? Why? Didn't you let me be a pirate?''

"Yes, but that's different. A robber is more high-class than a pirate, as a rule. In most countries they're of very high rank, lords and people like that.''

"Now, Tom, haven't you always been friendly to me? You wouldn't keep me out, would you, Tom? You wouldn't do that now, would you, Tom?''

"Huck, I wouldn't want to and I don't want to, but what would people say? Why, they'd say, 'H'm! Tom Sawyer's Gang! There are some very low-class fellows in it!' They'd mean you, Huck. You wouldn't like that, and I wouldn't.''

Huck was silent while a struggle was going on in his mind. Finally he said:

"Well, I'll go back to the widow for a month and see if I can bear it, if you'll let me join the gang, Tom.''

"All right, Huck, I agree! Come along, old fellow, and I'll ask the widow not to be so hard on you.''

"Will you, Tom, now will you? That's good of you. If she'll leave out some of the hardest things, I'll manage to live there or burst. When are you going to start the gang?''

"Oh, at once. We'll get the boys together and have the swearing-in to-night.''

"What's that?''

"It's to vow to stand by one another, and never tell

the gang's secrets, even if you're cut up into little bits."

"That's grand, Tom, that's really grand!"

"Isn't it? And all that swearing must be done at midnight, in the loneliest, awfullest place you can find. A haunted house is the best, but they're all dug up now."

"Well, midnight's good, anyway, Tom."

"Yes, so it is. And you've to swear on a coffin, and sign it with blood."

"Now, that's glorious! Why, it's a million times better than being a pirate! I'll stick to the widow till I die, Tom. And if I become a first-class robber, and everybody's talking about me, she'll be proud that she dragged me in out of the rain."

QUESTIONS

CHAPTER 1

1. Give examples of Tom's bad behaviour.
2. How did Aunt Polly try to make Tom behave well?

CHAPTER 2

1. Why did Jim take over an hour to fetch a bucket of water from the pump?
2. How did Tom make Ben eager to whitewash the fence?

CHAPTER 3

1. Why did Tom throw lumps of earth at Sid?
2 Why had Aunt Polly a troubled heart?

CHAPTER 4

1. How was the loose tooth pulled out?
2. What have you learnt about Huckleberry Finn from this chapter?

CHAPTER 5

1. Why did Tom march off from school?
2. What have you learnt from this chapter about Robin Hood?

CHAPTER 6

1. Why did (a) the boys, (b) the men, visit the graveyard at midnight?
2. Why did Dr. Robinson, Potter and Redskin Joe fight?

CHAPTER 7

1. What was the oath sworn by Tom and Huck, and why did they swear it?
2. Explain: "This last straw broke the camel's back."

CHAPTER 8

1. Why did people think that Potter had murdered Dr. Robinson?
2. Why did Tom sleep badly? Why did Sid sleep badly?

CHAPTER 9

1. Why was Tom as sad as a funeral? How did his aunt try to cure him?
2. Describe the different ways in which Pain-killer was used by both Aunt Polly and Tom.

CHAPTER 10

1. Describe Jackson's Island. Why did the boys choose it as a meeting-place?
2. How did conscience trouble Tom and Joe before they fell asleep?

CHAPTER 11

1. Describe what the boys saw on the river.
2. What did Tom do with the two pieces of bark?

CHAPTER 12

1. How did Tom get from the island to his aunt's house?
2. What did the villagers think when they found that the boys were missing?

CHAPTER 13

1. Describe briefly how the boys amused themselves on the island.
2. Why did Joe say to Tom, "I'll never speak to you again as long as I live"?

CHAPTER 14

1. How did the boys and their belongings suffer during and after the storm?
2. Explain: "Two of the Redskins almost wished that they had remained pirates."

CHAPTER 15

1. Why did the people in church rise to their feet and stare?
2. Why did Huck feel very uncomfortable?

CHAPTER 16

1. How did the boys get from the island to the village?
2. How did Tom make Becky jealous? How did Becky make Tom jealous?

CHAPTER 17

1. Why was Aunt Polly very angry when she returned from Mrs. Harper's?
2. Why did Aunt Polly cry with joy when she read the words which Tom had written on the piece of bark?

CHAPTER 18

1. Describe the part played in this chapter by Mr. Dobbins's book.
2. Why did Tom say that he tore the book?

CHAPTER 19

1. Describe the scene in the schoolroom while the mayor was presenting the first prize.
2. How did the boys obtain their revenge against the teacher?

CHAPTER 20

1. What was the evidence against Potter?
2. Why did Tom wish at night that he had not told the lawyer everything?

CHAPTER 21

1. When the boys failed to find any treasure, what reasons did Tom give?
2. Give a description of the haunted house.

CHAPTER 22

1. Describe the appearance of the Spaniard.
2. Why did Redskin Joe decide to go upstairs?

CHAPTER 28

1. What was Tom's plan to get the box of money?
2. Describe what Tom saw in Redskin Joe's room.

CHAPTER 24

1. Give a brief description of the picnic.
2. What did Huck overhear?

CHAPTER 25

1. What information about the two scoundrels did Huck obtain from the old Welshman?
2. How did the villagers try to find Tom and Becky?

CHAPTER 26

1. What made Tom and Becky wander into the depths of the cave?
2. Why were Tom and Becky unable to hurry towards the searchers whom they heard shouting?

CHAPTER 27

1 In what way were the children very lucky to escape from the cave?
2. Explain: " Nobody will get lost in that cave again."

CHAPTER 28

1. How did Tom discover where the box was hidden?
2. Give, in Mr. Jones's own words, the speech which he made at the party.

CHAPTER 29

1. Explain (a) Their sayings were treasured   (b) " Food comes too easily; I don't take any interest in it that way."
2. How did Tom persuade Huck to return to the Widow Douglas's?